SEDUCING
the
HEIRESS

MARTHA
KENNERSON

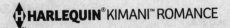

HARLEQUIN® KIMANI™ ROMANCE

Recycling programs
for this product may
not exist in your area.

ISBN-13: 978-0-373-86440-9

Seducing the Heiress

H HARLEQUIN®

Printed in U.S.A.

™ www.Harlequin.com

"Don't even think about it," Farrah said, clearly reading his intentions as she slowly backed away from him.

"Too late," Robert replied, backing her up against the elevator's wall. He placed his hands on both sides of her face, lowered his head and greedily took her mouth, as though everything in the kiss mattered to him, as though she mattered to him.

Farrah grabbed his shoulders and returned his kiss with just as much vigor. Robert managed to fight through the sexual haze and remember that this particular elevator wasn't private. Robert slowly released her mouth and stepped away from her. He was breathing hard and his sex was begging for release.

They stared at each other for several moments. Farrah raised her hand and placed her fingers across her swollen lips, which were quickly followed by her tongue.

"Damn it!" Robert started to step back to Farrah only to be stopped by the halt of the elevator. The doors opened and two men dressed in expensive-looking suits entered.

Robert stepped back and crossed his hands low in front of him, doing his best to hide the evidence of his desire.

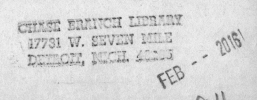

Dear Reader,

When I sat down and penned the first book in the Blake Sisters' series, I knew the story I wanted to tell. When the time came to write the second book in the series, the story took on a life of its own. The characters you'll meet are fun, sexy and determined to win... no matter what.

As a diehard fan of Harlequin romance books, I enjoy reading and writing stories that combine intrigue and a little deception in pursuit of romance. In *Seducing the Heiress*, Farrah and Robert fight an unknown enemy who is out to destroy their company, while trying to deny their intense passion for each other. The length that one of them takes to get what they want makes this game of cat and mouse a thrilling ride.

I thoroughly enjoy interacting with readers, so please let me know how you enjoyed Farrah and Robert's story. You can contact me on Facebook or Twitter. I look forward to bringing you Felicia Blake, the youngest sister's story, very soon.

Until next time,

Martha

Martha Kennerson's love of reading and writing is a significant part of who she is, and she uses both to create the kinds of stories that touch your heart. Martha lives with her family in League City, Texas, and believes her current blessings are only matched by the struggle it took to achieve such happiness. To find out more about Martha and her journey, check out her website at marthakennerson.com.

Books by Martha Kennerson

Harlequin Kimani Romance

Protecting the Heiress
Seducing the Heiress

Visit the Author Profile page at Harlequin.com for more titles.

This book is dedicated to the
Macro Literary All-Stars (M-LAS),
my writing support group. You're all amazing at what
you do and I'm happy we're taking this journey together.

Acknowledgments

I'd like to thank my King for putting romance in my heart
on a daily basis. Love you, baby.

Prologue

Farrah sat with her back against the tall white-pillowed headboard, holding the sheet to her chest with her right hand as she stared down at the diamond wedding band on her left hand.

"Unbelievable. I can't believe we did it… We actually did it."

"Which part?" Robert asked as he leaned over and kissed Farrah on an exposed shoulder, moving his way up her neck as he reached for the sheet. "Everything we did in the shower, or what you did to me on that mini-sofa thing by the window—that was my favorite, actually."

Farrah swatted Robert's hand away. "It's a settee, and that's not what I'm talking about. I'm talking about the fact that we're married."

"Oh, that," he said nonchalantly as his hand made its way under the cover, down her stomach and in between her thighs where he started stroking her core.

"Umm…yes…there…yes. Oh, no, you don't," she said, pushing his hand away and jumping out of the bed, wrapping the sheet around her body.

"Come back to bed, baby."

"No!" Farrah stared down at Robert's naked, erect body lying across the bed. "And I'd appreciate it if you put some clothes on so we can talk."

Robert sighed but complied. He reached for one of the plush white robes offered by the upscale hotel and wrapped it around his tall, muscular frame. "Better?"

"Much. We have to figure out how this even happened."

"We lost a bet and had to perform a dare."

"No, you lost the bet. Who asks for a hit while holding seventeen?" she questioned, tightening the sheet around her when she noticed his gaze lingered on one particular part of her anatomy.

"I was feeling lucky." Robert stood with his hands in the pockets, smiling down at Farrah. "I just knew that next card was a four. Anyway, Berkeley's your friend. Daring us to get married was her idea. Why would she do that?"

Farrah used her free hand to cover her face and shook her head. She sighed and dropped her hand. "When we were in law school, we made a bet about which one of us would marry first. You have to understand, we were both so ambitious…determined not to let anything or anyone stand in our way or prevent us from reaching our goals. Then we both fell in love, but ultimately got our hearts broken by those guys. So we made that bet—while we were both still nursing those broken hearts, mind you—as sort of a reminder. We were determined never to fall in love again and to focus only on our careers. When we finally started dating again, I guess we both figured that the other would give in first. It looks like she figured out a way to finally win the bet with this dare."

"That's a long time to hang on to a bet," Robert teased.

"We're lawyers. We don't forget anything, and we certainly never just let stuff go," she explained.

"You didn't have to go through with it, you know."

"Neither did you," she whispered, staring up into his eyes. He wet his lips, causing Farrah's nipples to harden against the sheet and creating a sensual pulsation at her core. They'd made love all night and all morning…and yet she still wanted more. "Besides, we were drunk. I didn't think they'd really marry us."

"This is Vegas. The home of quickie weddings. You signed the marriage license, I signed it, and that's all they needed." Robert pulled Farrah into his arms. "Why don't you let me take my beautiful wife out to lunch?"

Farrah's eyes widened slightly. "You know we can't stay married, right?" she asked, holding his gaze. "We have to get this taken care of before we return home Monday."

Robert's expression flowed from astonishment to revelation and finally determination. "Well, if all I've got is two days…" Robert dropped his robe and pulled the sheet from Farrah's body. "We'll order room service. I'm going to enjoy every bit of you while I can…and often."

Chapter 1

Farrah Blake completed her third conference call of the morning and was putting her phone away as she exited the elevator onto the twenty-first floor when she ran into the back of a tall, large male frame with a firm backside.

The second born of the highly accomplished Blake triplets, she held the position of corporate attorney and partner in her family's multibillion dollar international firm, which specialized in both corporate and personal security. "Excuse me," Farrah cried, stumbling back a couple of feet.

"No problem," a familiar baritone voice replied.

"Robert…" she said breathlessly. Farrah looked up to find the most beautiful set of blue eyes staring down at her just as he gifted her with a sexy smile. Farrah's body instantly responded to the sound, and her heart skipped several beats. Her nipples hardened and she throbbed at her core, a familiar occurrence that happened only with one man in particular.

Robert Gold, head of field security for Blake & Montgomery, could be summed up in three words: *handsome*, *wealthy* and extremely *sexy*. The fair-skinned, six-foot, athletically built computer genius had a well-earned reputation for being a playboy with a severe phobia of commitment and no desire to change his status, and now he was her husband because she'd lost a card game and had to perform a bet.

Farrah stood with her arms folded across her chest. "What are you doing here?"

"You know why I'm here," he said, giving her a megawatt smile that made most women melt on the spot. Farrah was definitely included in that number. She'd been fighting her growing desire for Robert since an out-of-town assignment had changed everything between them. Folks might claim that what happened in Vegas stayed in Vegas, but the memories were enough to have her waking up, breathing hard, wrapped in moist sheets.

"We talked about this already. You know that I'm more than capable of handling this on my own," Farrah declared as they made their way down the hall toward the most exclusive obstetrician and gynecologist's office in Houston.

She smiled and nodded as they passed two very expectant mothers who were having trouble keeping their balance, much like a couple of toddlers who were first learning to walk. "Wow," Farrah heard one of the women say; obviously she was admiring the view of Robert's backside, too. Farrah always thought pregnant women were beautiful, but seeing their struggle to stay upright, she was very grateful for her flat tummy and the ability to wear lime-green Betsey Johnson stilettos that set off her black-and-white formfitting Chanel dress perfectly. Determined to get her career back on track and her "lapse in judgment" in Vegas behind her, she had every intention of keeping it that way.

Robert's forehead creased, something that only happened when he was either deep in thought or really confused. "Is it me or are there far too many Halloween decorations up? Halloween's still three weeks away."

"Don't try to change the subject," Farrah scolded, stopping in the middle of the hallway, placing her right hand on her hip. "And no, there aren't. Look, we agreed that spending time alone together while we're still technically married wasn't a good idea, so we'd do our best to stay away from each other unless it's something business-related."

"No, *you* made that suggestion, and I've been ignoring it ever since," he said, falling in step beside her as they made it closer to the glass doors.

Farrah reached out and stopped his progress. "Look, I don't need you here with me. I'll let you know what happens." She glared up at him, trying to ignore her traitorous body and the feelings evoked by a simple touch. Farrah quickly dropped her hand.

"I'm not leaving. End of discussion," Robert stated, returning her angry look measure for measure.

Robert's handsome face and take-charge attitude were wreaking havoc on Farrah's senses. At the moment, she felt as though she would part her lips to speak, and all manner of nonsense would come tumbling out. What was it about this particular man that made her light-headed and giddy? She had to get away from him. Fast. Her sister needed her. "Like hell," she shot back, breaking eye contact. "Why are you being so unreasonable about this?"

Robert pushed out a deep breath. "Look, Meeks is my best friend and he may be neurotic as hell, but he's running late and he asked me to fill in until he arrives."

"I can take care of my sister very well, thank you very

much," Farrah said, trying to keep her temper and her body's responses under control.

"You sure we're in the right place?" Robert asked as they entered an opulent office setting filled with waiting mothers in various stages of developing motherhood.

The office of Dr. Erica Gunn, obstetrician and gynecologist to the rich and famous, was located in one of the most prestigious high-rise buildings in downtown Houston. Slate floors were covered in oriental rugs; soft leather seating was surrounded by wall-to-wall cathedral windows with breathtaking views of the city. The reception desk was fashioned from mahogany wood with intricate designs on its front. Farrah knew the desk was something her sister Francine, whose hobby was woodworking, must absolutely love. She smiled as she spied two of her company's agents diligently guarding the doors and eyeing their environment, while ignoring the admiring eyes of the female patients and staff. Somehow pregnant women had become dangerous? Sometimes her brother-in-law was too protective of Francine.

"Yep, right place." Robert gave a short nod to the two members from their team standing on high alert. "I should have expected Meeks to have backup."

Farrah made her way over to the receptionist's desk.

"Pardon me. I'm looking for my sister Francine Blake... I mean Montgomery, Francine Montgomery," Farrah corrected, inwardly chiding herself to get it right. The couple had been married for nearly a year, but Francine had been the fiercely overprotective eldest triplet that relished being the leader of their little pack for so long, it was still hard to concede that she now belonged to someone else.

"Still not quite used to your sister's new name, I see. At least my last name wasn't the only one you couldn't get used to," Robert said in a tone so harsh it sent a shiver of unease down Farrah's spine.

"Seriously? What are you doing?" Farrah asked, scanning the seated patrons to make sure no one had overheard his comments.

"What am I...?" Robert pushed out another deep breath as though he was in need of a woosah moment to keep his emotions under control. "I'm not the one freaking out about the possibility of someone finding out we're married."

"We won't be married much longer. Besides, our mistake is no one's business," she whispered. "Evidently, we had both taken leave of our senses."

Robert held her gaze for several moments before his piercing blue eyes swept over her body, making her breasts heavy and all her blood rush south to the one place it didn't need to settle. "No, our *mistake* is no one's business," he conceded, and the deflated sound of his voice caused a dull pain in Farrah's chest.

"Sorry about that. How can I..." the receptionist said after she disconnected the call and looked up at Farrah. Her voice trailed off as her eyes grew wide, taking in the woman standing in front of the desk.

The response was one that was all too familiar to Farrah, as one-third of a set of triplets. Olive-skinned beauties with high cheekbones and expressive eyes inherited from their Italian mother and the luxuriously long jet-black hair, straight noses and heart-shaped faces bestowed on them from their African-American and Hispanic father, the three women were only set apart by distinctive eye colors.

"Oh, my goodness," she said in an anxious whisper. "You look just like Mrs. Montgomery. Except for the baby bump, of course."

"Thank goodness for that," Farrah murmured, instinctively placing her hand on the place where a child would grow one day…in the very distant future. Right now she had a career to salvage and a "never should have been a husband" to extract from her life.

Robert cut his eyes to her, which she did her best to ignore, while her treacherous body continued to betray her with all manner of foolishness. "I'm here for my sister's ultrasound. She's expecting me."

"*We're* here for the ultrasound…Karen," Robert corrected, smiling down at the young woman and reading her name tag.

Karen's smile grew wide and she flipped her brown wavy hair off her shoulder in a move Farrah clearly recognized. *If she smiles any wider, I'll be able to count every tooth in her head.* Farrah frowned at the other woman who had suddenly found a pointed interest in the male part of the equation.

"Yes, Mrs. Montgomery is expecting both of you," she said to Robert in a voice that had clearly taken on a more seductive tone. "She told us her sister and a family friend would be joining her and her husband whenever he arrives. That's when she also felt the need to explain about the armed security that actually searched the entire place before parking themselves here in the waiting area."

Farrah tried to hold in a frustrated sigh, but her efforts didn't escape Robert's notice.

"Oh, no worries," the receptionist said. "The majority of our clientele requires the same kind of security. It's nothing new to us. I assume you're that family friend and *not* the husband…right?" she inquired, directing her question to Robert.

Robert gifted Karen with a wide smile of his own and that legendary charm automatically kicked into high gear. "Yes… I'm definitely not *her* husband," he answered before giving Farrah a hard look. "Nor, for that matter, am I considered anyone else's."

Farrah experienced such an intense and unexpected jab of jealousy and possessiveness watching the exchange, she found herself inching closer to Robert. Before she knew it, common sense took a road trip to never-never land as she parted her lips and said, "No, he's not my sister's husband. He's mine."

Chapter 2

"So much for not sharing our business," Robert murmured to Farrah, returning the smirk she'd given their shocked, starry-eyed receptionist.

Farrah ignored his comments, finding a more pointed interest in the concerned look of one of their staff members that was within earshot of their conversation. Karen's right hand flew to her heart. "Oh, your sister hadn't mentioned anything about a brother-in-law."

"I'm sure she didn't," Robert said sarcastically, adding, "She can't share what she doesn't know."

Farrah hadn't thought through her rash decision to share that bit of information with the receptionist. She offered Robert a defiant stare before turning back to the young woman. "We're very private people," Farrah explained, all signs of that smirk gone. "I'm sure you understand and will respect our privacy."

"Of course...please excuse me just one moment and

I'll take you both back," Karen replied as she turned to address a man that had been hovering nearby but was now approaching her, holding several files with a confused look on his face.

Robert turned and leaned against the desk. "So *now* you want to share the fact that we're married."

"Will you please lower your voice?" Farrah scolded, scanning the faces of the mothers-to-be who were sharing glances that she was certain had everything to do with them.

"You can't have it both ways, you know," he said, narrowing his gaze on her flushed face. "Just because you're jealous—"

"I'm not jealous," she snapped through a forced smile. "And I'm certainly *not* the one who was sneaking around trying to find out what's going on between me and Trey Steel, who wouldn't even be here if it weren't for you."

Tremaine Steel, often called Trey by his family and friends, was a wealthy senior partner in his family's exceptionally successful law firm, and had become involved in defending Blake & Montgomery in a patent lawsuit. He had a reputation for being a talented attorney who loved the ladies. From what Robert had learned about the man, his looks, deep pockets and wicked charm could make a woman drop to her knees. The report on Robert's desk spoke to the fact that plenty of them had done just that, and a lot more, on more than one occasion.

Blake & Montgomery had been entangled in a lawsuit over the ownership of a security patent for a single-system digital device that would incorporate all of one's personal and business security needs for the past five years.

Ted Jefferson Jr., the son of a deceased former business partner of the firm's founders, Frank Blake and Milton Montgomery, was claiming that it was his father's original drawings and specs on which Robert had based his ideas for a revolutionary new security system that would allow users to secure their home, business and digital information using fingerprint and palm-recognition technology.

Farrah had played a vital role in developing their defense from the moment she joined the company, and within the last two years had become the lead attorney on the case. Although the lower courts had offered a judgment in their favor, Blake & Montgomery was being forced to defend itself in both the media and through the court's appeals process.

Robert had requested and gained the board's support to bring in an outside attorney to take over the case through the next phase of its defense, especially since it was his own program designs that were at the center of the dispute. Strangely enough, a furious Farrah had decided not to fight the board on the matter. Instead she insisted on being a part of the attorney selection process. That should have been his tip-off that she was up to something. Farrah's selection of Tremaine Steel was an exceptional choice happily accepted by all concerned— almost all.

Tremaine Steel had successfully argued cases before both the State and Federal Supreme Courts, which made him the perfect person to handle the Blake & Montgomery patent appeal. But as far as Robert was concerned, he had better steer clear of Farrah, or Robert might find himself in need of an attorney of his own for a far different reason.

"I wasn't sneaking around doing anything," Robert protested. "I may have inquired a few times as to what was going on with the case." He ran his right hand through his hair. "Look, we've talked about this already. You know that I think you're an amazing attorney. It's just, with all the different types of claims being leveled…"

Farrah twisted her neck around and her eyebrows flew up.

"Wait," Robert raised his hands in surrender, trying to hold off the scolding he knew was coming. "Not that you don't know what you're doing."

"Whatever," she said, giving him a dismissive wave. "You got what you wanted. Just stay out of my business from now on. We certainly don't need a repeat of Vegas."

Vegas. Ah, Vegas. How could he forget?

Farrah was winding through the casino floor of the MGM Grand Hotel, trying to block all the noise—bells, cheers of joy and tears of disappointment—preparing to enter the unseasonably warm April weather, when she saw Robert Gold heading her way. "What are you doing here?"

"Meeks sent me to help you."

"To settle a contract dispute? How exactly do you plan to help me do that?"

He shrugged. "In any way you need."

"Go home, Robert," Farrah shot back as she moved around him and continued toward the exit.

Robert followed her outside, pulling his aviator sunglasses down from his head and over his eyes. "Look, I'm here to stay, so you might as well put me to work."

Farrah reached into her bag and pulled out a document and a certified check. "It's already done," she said, handing him the document and placing a pair of Chanel sunglasses over those sexy siren eyes.

Robert put his right arm over Farrah's shoulders and smiled. "Well, in that case, it's the weekend, so let's play." For two people who had been dancing around the edges of friendship and passion since she'd joined the family business, play, *which included a lot of tequila,*

*was the operative word. Marriage happened to be the
unexpected endgame.*

"For the millionth time, I didn't crash your Vegas trip,"
Robert insisted. "Meeks sent me to help."

"Help I didn't need," she shot back, rubbing her temple.
"Look, it's just…"

"Just what? Finish your thought," he demanded.

Farrah moved to the corner of the room and Robert
enjoyed the wonderful view as he followed on her heels.
She turned and faced him. "You shouldn't be flirting in
front of me. At least not until after our divorce is final.
You should have more respect for me and our marriage,
no matter how short-lived it may be. Is that too much
to ask?"

"Respect for a marriage you claimed was a mistake,"
he replied. "One you can't get out of fast enough—is that
the marriage we're talking about? The one you want me
to *respect*?" Robert said through his teeth with his fist
clenched at his side as he fought for control. Why couldn't
she see what they had—could still have—was special?
Why did it have to end up like a cliché?

They stared at each other in silence. Robert had never
wanted a woman as much as he wanted Farrah. Not even
the betrayal by his college sweetheart that had made him
swear off serious relationships could compare to what he
felt for Farrah. He adored everything about her. From the
way she challenged and pushed him to her fierce and protective love for her family. Standing this close, he could
smell the scent of her favorite vanilla shampoo and it,
along with the sexy dress that draped her body like a
second skin, sent his body on high alert.

Farrah lowered her head and shook it slowly. "We had
a little too much to drink in *Vegas*." She lifted her head
to meet his gaze. "We got married on a dare. At some

cheesy little spot called the Tunnel of Love Chapel," she said in a voice barely above a whisper. "Who does that?"

Robert clamped down on his factual answer that it happened more times than people liked to give credit.

"You bet it was a mistake," she continued. "Hell, we *both* agreed it was a mistake."

Robert sighed and nodded. He had agreed that marrying the way they had—at a drive-through window—was a mistake, but he was convinced that the marriage itself wasn't one at all. An awareness he'd come to *after* realizing his friendly feelings for Farrah had developed into something deeper and irrevocable. The thought that she could be showing some serious interest in Tremaine Steel made his need to convince Farrah that they belonged together much more urgent.

"That reminds me. Have you heard from Fletcher?" she asked. "He has filed the papers, right?"

Fletcher Scott was the private detective turned lawyer they often used when they didn't want their agency directly involved in certain cases, mostly for "personal" activities. A secret marriage and quickie divorce didn't get any more personal. Farrah was very thankful that Fletcher could keep a secret, even from her sisters.

"Yes, the papers have definitely been filed," Robert assured, while thinking, *Sort of...*

"Good!" she said on a relieved sigh. "We've put this off long enough."

Robert and Farrah walked back to the reception desk as soon as they heard Meeks's voice. "I'm Meeks Montgomery and I'm—"

"Yes, your wife's been asking for you," Karen said, smiling as she flipped her hair again.

Both Robert and Meeks wore the Blake & Montgomery standard uniform of a black T-shirt with their company's red logo that was hard to miss. Robert was accustomed to female attention when wearing it, especially since the uniform showed off his broad shoulders and flat chest and abs. Also, the combat boots and a utility belt holding a nine-millimeter handgun that screamed *dangerous* were hard to miss. And even his ninety-year-old neighbor had a liking for the black cargo pants that showcased a rear end she tried sneaking a squeeze of on occasion. Robert didn't have the heart to tell the old woman that he was onto her game. The devilish smile that plastered her wrinkled face was too endearing.

Evidently, the geriatric club wasn't the only group that wasn't immune. Karen's breathing had increased and she'd flipped her hair—yet again. The corner of Robert's mouth curved up. He'd always enjoyed the attention he received from women, especially if said attention seemed to bother the only woman he ever really wanted. Meeks, on the other hand, didn't seem to take notice of anyone other than his wife. So Robert was in good company.

"If you'd all come this way," she said.

"Ladies first," Robert chimed, stepping aside so Farrah could move past.

"Such a gentleman," Farrah shot back.

"You should know that nothing could be further from the truth," he answered with a knowing wink.

Farrah huffed, but didn't come back with her normal biting retort. They followed Karen through a set of double doors and down a well-lit hall with white marble floors and white walls into another small waiting area. The room had walls painted light gray, with pictures and posters that centered on pregnancy, and was filled with low-back gray leather chairs.

"You two will need to wait here, and someone will

come for you when they're ready to start the ultrasound," she said to both Farrah and Robert.

They both acknowledged her request with a small nod.

"Follow me, Mr. Montgomery. I'll take you to your wife."

"I'll see you two in a bit," Meeks said before giving them both a lengthy once-over and asking, "Are you two okay?"

"Yes, why do you ask?" Farrah said, her red lips pulled into a scowl.

"If I didn't know any better," Meeks said, tilting his head, "I swear you two were acting like a married couple in the middle of a fight."

"You don't say," Robert teased, garnering an angry glare from Farrah.

Meeks shook his head and continued down the hall. Both Robert and Farrah took a seat next to each other. "I guess now we wait," Robert said.

"I guess so," Farrah agreed as she sat and crossed her legs. Her dress rose a few inches, offering Robert a view of Farrah's thighs—a move that he could have done without. Now he was imagining what delightful things Farrah had on under that shape-defining dress. He knew first hand that she spared no expense when it came to buying and wearing beautiful, soft and sensual underwear. Robert's sex grew hard as steel.

Robert quickly flicked his wrist and checked his watch, then pulled out his phone and sorted through a few emails.

"We passed an area with a coffee and vending machine on our way in here. You want something?" Farrah asked, getting to her feet.

He couldn't actually say that what he wanted was the woman herself.

"I can get it," Robert said, putting away his phone.

"I need to stretch my legs," Farrah insisted.

"If you insist, sure, coffee would be fine. You know how I like it…strong and hot," he teased, staring up at her, his face expressionless. The sexual tension between them was choking him.

Before Farrah could make a move toward the door, a male nurse stepped to them. "They're ready for you," he said.

Robert rose from his chair, slowly, discreetly making an attempt to adjust himself. He took a deep breath and released it slowly. "You ready?" Robert finally asked, offering his hand.

Farrah nodded slowly as her eyes darted away from the reason he had clearly needed a moment. He was too turned on to be embarrassed. Hell, the woman was practically his wife. More like actually his wife—and he intended to keep it that way.

"Let's go," Robert said as they followed behind the nurse.

After Francine's appointment, Farrah thanked the male nurse that guided them to a different set of elevators. "Sorry about the inconvenience, but the contractors have started roping off the front area of the office," he explained.

"It's fine," Farrah reassured.

Farrah smiled as she stood next to Robert waiting for the doors to open. "That was—"

"Intense is what that was," Robert supplied as he reached and pushed the down button.

"Yes, it was," Farrah agreed, pulling out a compact and flipping it open to check her reflection.

Robert's voice was a sultry whisper as he said, "You look beautiful…as always."

"Thank you," Farrah said, smiling up at him. "At least my eyes aren't swollen from all that crying. I didn't know that I would feel that way."

"They looked very calm, too," Robert said and this time his tone had shifted to shock. "I'm not sure how I'd be able to handle such a surprise."

"It wasn't that much of a surprise," Farrah explained. "We've always known that it was a possibility that one or all of us could have multiple babies at once. Francine just happens to be the first to prove that theory correct."

"Twins…wow," Robert said as a sudden vibration of his phone snatched his attention.

Farrah locked in on Robert's profile and commanding presence. An image of two tiny babies, both with crystal-blue eyes, one with jet-black curly hair and the other sandy brown with blond highlights, flashed into Farrah's mind.

Vegas. Marriage. Divorce. Life without Robert… uncharted territory. Farrah knew Robert wasn't a long-term, forever type of guy—his history proved that— so why was she imagining what their future kids could look like? Suddenly, for no reason she could explain, her heart ached.

Chapter 3

"Everything's set for our trip," Robert said, hitting the send button on his cell phone after replying to his assistant's text message. He reached and hit the elevator call button.

"Good, I have a couple of things to wrap up before we leave for New York," Farrah explained.

"You don't have to go with me, you know. I'm sure we'll just be chasing another dead end. Alexia covered her tracks well." Robert turned to face Farrah and jammed his hands in his pockets to keep from reaching out and smoothing her hair away from her beautiful face.

Alexia Gray, a former employee of Blake & Montgomery, had been hired as a senior-level attorney for their corporate legal team. Through a complaint, Robert discovered that Alexia had made several attempts to blackmail their clients with the same information that they'd been hired to protect. She was arrested and currently sat in the county jail awaiting trial on multiple charges. However, before she was caught, Alexia had been hired to alter key design schematics that made it appear that Robert's ideas and designs weren't his own—an alteration that appeared to substantiate the charges against the firm, allowing an appeal to move forward, a fact that had only recently been discovered.

Alexia refused to provide them with the necessary proof to clear their names, get the bogus lawsuit against Blake & Montgomery dismissed and permit them to move forward with production, forcing Robert and Farrah to track down the person who'd hired her to sabotage their filing and ultimately their company.

"We agreed to work this case together no matter what or where it leads us." Farrah adjusted her purse on her shoulder. "This elevator sure is slow. Besides, you'd look out of place attending a Broadway show alone, no matter how good you may look in a tux," she said, giving him that smile that could melt snow.

"I still don't get why we have to sit through a Broadway play just to find out information about Alexia's clients," Robert complained.

"A little culture won't kill you," Farrah teased, chuckling at his scowl. "Not everyone's into extreme testosterone-fueled activities—base-jumping, free-hand mountain climbing—"

"High-stakes gambling," Robert offered, snickering.

Farrah glared at him through narrowed eyes. "We have to find out who she's working with, and from all the information I've been able to gather, the common denominator seems to be this play. She thought it was the perfect cover."

"Who uses a play as a cover for corporate sabotage?"

"According to more than one of my informants, not to

mention all the playbills we found in Alexia's apartment, *she* seems to do exactly that," she said.

"I find it ironic that she chose *Chicago* for this particular activity, don't you?" he asked.

"Not…really," she said, frowning.

"All the women in the play are criminals," he said, laughing. "You don't find that ironic?"

"Not at all. She's a criminal. She can relate," Farrah said, shrugging. "And since the firm is in the business of putting criminals behind bars, as well as protecting people, it's not ironic to us, either."

The back office elevator doors finally opened and they were met by a wall of mahogany wood with raised panels, a wood tray ceiling with a small crystal chandelier and dark travertine tile floors. Although this elevator didn't have a red velvet sofa and carpeted floors, it was a sight that was very familiar to them. As soon as they stepped inside, it was as if they were transported back in time to a place where they were wrapped in a familiar blanket of desire. They looked at each other and smiled; clearly they were both remembering the last time they'd been in a similar tight situation together. When they'd finally stopped fighting their desire for each other.

"This is one of the owners' private elevators. It opens into his personal suite. Why do you have a key?" Farrah asked, giving Robert a mischievous smile.

"Because I happen to be one of those owners," Robert replied, leaning against the elevator wall, while admiring the sexy strapless red mini dress and sky-high heels she wore. He reached over and pushed the stop button on the vintage elevator panel.

Farrah opened her mouth to protest but quickly closed it. Within seconds, the phone that was concealed behind a wooden panel rang. Robert kept his eyes on Farrah while picking up the receiver. "Stand down, everything's fine," he said before disconnecting. "Got to love Vegas security."

Robert closed the short distance between them, trapping Farrah between the wall of the elevator and his wide chest. Farrah raised her chin and the movement caused her breasts to rise—showing off her cleavage as she gifted him with that slow sexy smile he loved. He leaned forward and rested the palms of his hands against the wall to brace himself. Farrah rose up on the tips of her toes, circled her arms around Robert's neck and kissed him. Her taste ignited something inside of him and Robert returned the kiss with far more passion than he'd intended.

Lost in the moment, Robert took his right hand and reached under Farrah's dress. He ripped off the thin piece of lace and string she called panties, placed it in his jacket pocket and started stroking her core with the tips of two fingers. He stared into her eyes and watched as she fell to pieces in his hand. Robert moved in closer, placing a gentle kiss on her forehead, then lowered a few inches to devour Farrah's lips before he brought those same fingers to his mouth and kissed off her essence. "Delicious," he said as he watched her dilated pupils widen.

"I'll be the judge of that," Farrah said in a voice barely above a whisper before capturing his lips into another passionate kiss. "Hmm...."

Robert picked Farrah up and carried her the two feet to the velvet sofa placed against the back wall of the elevator. He sat with Farrah straddled across his lap. "Wife," he whispered in her ear.

"Husband," she replied.

The elevator stopped, releasing them from the past,

and they both stood in silence as the doors opened to no one. The doors closed again and Robert turned to face Farrah. The dress she wore may have been different and the environment not exactly the same, but Robert's desire for Farrah was stronger than ever.

"Don't even think about it," Farrah said, clearly reading his intentions as she slowly backed away from him.

"Too late," Robert replied, backing her up against the elevator's wall. He placed his hands on both sides of her face, lowered his head and greedily took her mouth, as though everything in the kiss mattered to him, as though *she* mattered to him.

Farrah grabbed his shoulders and returned his kiss with just as much vigor. Robert managed to fight through the sexual haze and remember that this particular elevator wasn't private. Robert slowly released her mouth and stepped away from her. He was breathing hard and his sex was begging for release.

They stared at each other for several moments. Farrah raised her hand and placed her fingers across her swollen lips, which were quickly followed by her tongue.

"Damn it!" Robert started to step back to Farrah only to be stopped by the halt of the elevator. The doors opened and two Hispanic men dressed in expensive-looking suits entered.

Robert stepped back and crossed his hands low and in front of him, doing his best to hide the evidence of his desire.

"Second floor, please," one of the men said to Robert. who was standing next to the control panel.

"No problem," Robert replied, pressing the button with his elbow, causing one of the men to take a swift look at Farrah, then back to Robert's strategically placed hands.

"Looks like we should have taken the next one," the shorter of the two men teased, causing Farrah to blush.

The doors opened to the second floor and both men took their exit without any further comment.

"Farrah—"

"No!" she said, using her hand to halt his words. "Please don't."

The elevator doors opened to the ground floor. Farrah smoothed out her dress, raised her chin and walked out of the elevator.

"See you later," Farrah called back over her shoulder.

"Sooner than you think," Robert murmured as he watched her take her leave. Robert pulled out his phone and placed a call that he'd hoped he wouldn't have to make so soon. "Fletcher... Robert Gold. Farrah's getting anxious, so it's time to move forward with Plan B."

"You sure about this, man? Why not just tell her the truth?" Fletcher asked.

"She's not ready for the truth just yet, but hopefully soon she will be."

"If you say so, but I'd better not lose my license over this. She's a damn good attorney with a sharp legal mind and an impeccable reputation," Fletcher said, his concern evident—as well it should be. Farrah was also known for her prominent list of contacts, long memory and ability to hold a grudge—something that made Robert's plan all that more dangerous.

"I know, but don't worry about it. If things go south, I'll take all the blame. Just bring all the necessary paperwork to my office in the morning." Robert pulled his car keys from his pocket and started his car so the air conditioning would kick in by the time he got in.

"If you're sure, I'll see you first thing in the morning?" Fletcher asked, obviously needing one final reassurance.

"I'm sure. Losing Farrah isn't an option...no matter what I have to do," Robert said, disconnecting the call.

"I hope I haven't kept you waiting too long," Trey said, offering Farrah a wide smile that showed off a set of deep dimples as he reached for her hand.

Farrah stood. "Not at all. I just arrived." His large hand engulfed hers and she smiled and sighed at his touch, but the confident and satisfied look on Trey's face told her he'd obviously gotten the wrong idea. Yes, she found him attractive; what red-blooded woman wouldn't? The tall, muscularly built litigator with smooth, milk-chocolate skin and sexy dark eyes would complete most women's must-have list, but his touch only confirmed what she already knew. No one's touch could affect her like Robert's— a fact she wasn't ready to deal with—which also had her quickly extracting her hand from Trey's. At some point, Farrah had to put her feelings for Robert in their proper perspective, but it wouldn't happen on the heels of her falling into the arms of another man.

"Please follow me." Trey led Farrah through the lobby of Steel & Associates, which left no doubt that she was dealing with a successful and very expensive firm. If the eighty-first floor location in one of Houston's most expensive buildings wasn't enough of a hint, the expensive furnishings and artwork most certainly would be.

"Are you okay? You look a little flushed."

"I'm fine." Farrah felt slightly embarrassed, as she was still reeling from the effects of Robert's kiss and the fact that she'd acted like a shameless hussy and gone all in for that kiss like a wanton woman.

"Have a seat. Can I get you anything to drink?" Trey asked.

"No, thanks." Farrah took a place at the conference

table near the door and slid open a set of documents he had prepared. "So, what have you and your team determined?"

Trey took the chair next to Farrah. "That not only are you beautiful but you're an exceptional attorney."

The compliment made her smile, but his sensual tone was off-putting.

"I don't see why they brought me in on this in the first place."

"It certainly wasn't my idea," she murmured, her eyes still on the document before her.

"Hmm. Mr. Control?"

"Mr. Control?" she questioned, looking up from the page.

"Robert Gold," he said. Farrah returned her eyes to her document. "It sounds like he might have some doubt in your ability where there shouldn't be. So far, we haven't seen anything that makes me think you missed anything with your initial filing, and that your response is on point, with one exception."

Farrah lifted her gaze again from the document that had captured her attention and locked it on him. "And that would be what, exactly?" she asked, tilting her head slightly.

"That's what I admire most about you, Farrah. Your confidence." His dark brown eyes narrowed in on her. "You can't even *imagine* that you might have missed something or could be going in the wrong direction, can you?"

"I worked every possible line of defense in my mind before I even committed it to paper. If you have something to say, Trey, spit it out," she demanded.

"In a nutshell, your response to the lawsuit is that Robert Gold's plans are based solely on his own work product and not anything that has been provided, past or present, by the complainant," Trey explained.

"Correct."

"Yet, you offer no proof." He leaned forward, resting his forearms against the edge of the table. "We need something to substantiate that…something that counters what they've presented or could potentially present."

Inwardly, she chuckled. "I realize that, and we're working on it," she replied, understanding that she had been so busy holding her cards close to the chest that she hadn't considered that Trey needed another piece of vital information. "We're in the process of trying to find whoever's behind all this as well as the forger that created the forged drawings that they used in their complaint document."

Trey sat upright quickly, surprise evident in his expression. "Are you now? And what happens if you don't?"

She closed her eyes a moment, and flashed through every possible scenario and summed it up with, "To be perfectly honest? We're screwed… *I'm* screwed."

Trey's full lips lifted in a small smile. "No, you're not. I have my team checking on a few more angles for us to explore. Have dinner with me so we can talk through all the options and opportunities before us."

The only "angle" Trey Steel wanted to work was the horizontal tango. "Really, Trey? You throw in a cheesy pickup line when you ask me to a working dinner? Where'd you learn that? Caveman Practices 101?"

"A brother's got to try."

"Not really," Farrah said, laughing. "You can try, just not with me."

"But a sister also has to eat," he hedged.

"Thanks, but I have other plans already. Why don't

you just email your ideas and I'll take a look at what you have in mind?"

"Rain check?" he asked with one raised eyebrow.

"Let's just focus on the response." Farrah got up and headed to the door.

"I never give up, you know," Trey declared, and she recognized it for the challenge he meant it to be.

"Of course I know," she shot back. "That's why we became attorneys in the first place."

His laughter followed her from the conference room.

Chapter 4

Farrah drove into the underground garage of the Blake & Montgomery office building and parked in her assigned space. She turned off the ignition and laid her head back against the headrest of her new white Porsche 911 Turbo Coupe. Farrah believed in working hard so she could play equally hard, which meant having some really cool toys—fast cars, a beautiful boat and vacation homes all over the world. Her most recent purchase was a prime piece of real estate in Paris, France, with views the length of the Champs-Élysées to the Arc de Triomphe.

Farrah pushed up her sun visor and caught a glimpse of her image in its mirror. The sight of her lips summoned the memory of the kiss she'd shared with Robert. "What the hell's wrong with you? This is exactly why you have to either learn to control yourself or stay the hell away from him," she said to her reflection.

She noted that Robert's car was missing from its space.

They drove the same kind of Porsche, but his was a startling black. He, too, had a thing for enjoying life and a few expensive toys. Something that should make them gravitate toward one another, but his capacity to make her feel inadequate about her work was the very thing that drove her away. She couldn't understand why he didn't just trust her ability to handle their court case to its end.

Farrah exited the car, entered their building and made her way to the floor where the administrative offices of Blake & Montgomery were located. In addition to their company, their building housed her and her sister's personal residences as well as several additional apartments. Farrah walked past the midlevel cubicles as she headed to her office after being stopped only once.

Farrah's office was designed exactly like her sister's, only her furnishings were less traditional and more contemporary. A large oval-shaped curly-redwood desk with a turquoise inlay was the focal point of the room. There was also a six-seat, round curly-redwood conference table with red leather high-back chairs, and bookshelves that held a mixture of books and antique art pieces. In a corner stood a small, fully stocked bar and an antique hidden safe.

She had just powered up her computer when her office door flew open and only partly closed, allowing Paul White, the Blake sisters' part-time stylist, to make a dramatic entrance.

"Where have you been? I've been dying here. How did Francine's ultrasound go?" Paul asked, excitement written all over his clean-shaven face as he placed an electronic tablet and coffee cup on Farrah's desk. He used his hand to brush his curly black hair from his face.

Paul also happened to hold the title of Francine and Farrah's assistant, best friend and unofficial brother.

They'd been friends throughout grade school and when Paul's family abandoned him after he came out his sopho-more year of college, the Blake family had welcomed him with open arms, making his college years less lonely—his words exactly.

"You need a haircut," Farrah said.

"I know. What happened?"

"You mean she hasn't called you yet?" Farrah said, frowning as she leaned back in the Herman Miller chair.

"Yeah, she called while I was on the phone taking care of everything for your New York trip, so she had to leave me a message." Paul slipped his tall, lean frame into the chair across from Farrah's desk—his favorite spot. "All she said was that she had 'big news' and that she'd call me later because she was taking the rest of the day off to celebrate with Meeks. So…" Paul's hazel eyes had widened and he was rotating his index finger. "Spill. What are they celebrating?"

Paul leaned in, eyebrows rising in comedic fashion.

"The ultrasound revealed that…" She paused for dramatic effect.

"Woman, don't make me kill you up in this fancy office of yours!"

"They're having twins—a boy and girl."

Paul flew out of his chair and started dancing around the room. "Yes! Yes! Yes!"

At that moment, Robert's face flashed through her mind again, and she felt a pain in her chest that she didn't dare give a name. Would she have been happy if she'd gotten news that she was carrying Robert's child? Would they share doctor's appointments, quarrel over baby names before compromising over the best ways to prepare to bring their child into the world? *No, that can't be. What's wrong with you?* Why was he always in her thoughts these days?

"Thank goodness," Paul said with a relived sigh. "I figured it had to be something. I just knew she shouldn't be that big already."

"Really, Paul… Really?"

"What?"

Farrah shook her head, welcoming their banter to distract her from thoughts of her soon-to-be ex-that-no-one-knew.

Paul gave a dismissive wave and sat back down. "Francine's body changing that much because she's having twins is one thing. Gaining weight for no reason other than she decided to let herself go is something else." Paul picked up his cup and took several sips.

"You act like she's as big as a house or something." Farrah turned her attention back to her computer, but couldn't help grinning at the mental image of her sister's rounded belly and the smile and happiness that seemed to accompany Francine everywhere she went these days.

Paul took a swig of his coffee. "Girl, Francine's four months and she looks like she's six or seven."

"She's five months and she's the perfect weight for an expectant mother of twins," she corrected, choosing not to look directly into Paul's face.

Paul tilted his head slightly. "What's wrong? Why do you seem a little…off?" he asked, frowning as he returned the cup to its former place.

Farrah's hand automatically flew to her mouth as though her lips could tell the story all by themselves. *Damn, you act like somebody's parent. You notice everything, even the slightest change.*

"Did you and Robert have a quickie before coming in

today?" he asked, grinning and wiggling his eyebrows in a manner that sent a shiver of unease up her spine.

Farrah got up and went to close her door completely. "Keep your voice down. And no, we didn't just have a quickie."

Farrah returned to her desk and looked fiercely back at Paul, who was eyeing her suspiciously.

"What?" she asked holding out her hands and hunching her shoulders.

"You tell me," he said in a serious tone she wasn't used to hearing from him. Paul had once been very serious... too serious. He'd spent years fighting and hiding who he really was and he'd nearly lost himself in the process. Paul's relationship with the Blake sisters and their family, as well as finding love and marrying his partner John in a lavish ceremony hosted by his new sisters, had kept Paul's love for life alive and his heart light.

Farrah looked down at her bare left hand and slowly shook her head.

They both sat in silence for several minutes before Paul reminded Farrah of something that she already knew. "Everyone needs a go-to person to confide in, and I know that's your sisters, but for some reason you've chosen to share this secret with me—"

Farrah looked up. "You know you're like a brother to us," she affirmed emphatically.

"Then talk to your brother. What's wrong, Big Sis?" he asked, leaning forward, taking both her hands into his.

Farrah closed her eyes, took a deep breath and released it slowly. She slowly opened her eyes and said, "Robert kissed me after we left the doctor's office."

"So?" Paul said, with a bewildered expression.

"So!" Farrah said, pulling her hands free. "Have you not been listening to me all those times we've discussed this? Paul, the man's kisses are earth-shattering. If we hadn't been interrupted, I would have let him take me right there in the elevator…again."

Paul grinned. "Earth-shattering!" A small laugh escaped before he clamped a hand over his mouth.

Farrah glared at him. Paul often enjoyed her rare moments of insanity. "It's not funny. I mean, it's like I'm under some type of spell whenever he trains those beautiful blue eyes on me." Just the thought had certain parts of her body coming to attention. And right now, she couldn't afford to have anyone getting that attention…she had work to do.

"Why are you fighting this thing between you two so hard? You want him and he's obviously crazy about you."

"Yeah, right now…*maybe*. We both know how quickly his interest in women can change, how his eyes begin to wander…not to mention everything else—his lips, hands, his…"

Paul's eyes widened to the size of golf balls.

"Sorry, TMI. Besides, we're too much alike and we want different things."

"Do you? Like what? Because the way I see it, you want the exact same things. I mean, you both love what you do, you love to travel, and you spend money on crazy expensive toys—"

"Like what?" Farrah demanded, sitting up straight in her chair.

"Like that old-ass gun you spent fifteen thousand dollars on last month," he said with a raised eyebrow.

"It was an antique that's already increased in value," she defended. "So it's an investment."

"Yeah, like the *antique* double ceiling fan that Robert bought for his office a couple of weeks ago. How much did he spend on that thing?"

"Ten thousand dollars, but it was a great deal. And it has also increased in value," she explained.

"See what I mean. Something else you have in common, spending money on old…" She raised an eyebrow and he quickly amended, "I mean, antique stuff you really don't need."

Farrah stood and looked out her window at the view of downtown Houston. "Robert and I wouldn't be together long-term and I won't risk…"

"You won't risk what…your heart?" In the silence that ensued, Paul left the chair and came to stand next to Farrah at the window and snaked his right arm around her waist.

Farrah laid her head on his shoulder. "Girlfriend, you have to be willing to risk everything if you want everything in return," he said in a voice barely above a whisper.

Farrah rifled through a set of scenarios of how that would work, how she'd manage physical compatibility without mutual trust. Regardless of how she might feel about Robert, it just wasn't enough. "No…not with Robert. He was crazy in love once and got his heart handed to him."

Paul gasped and Farrah raised her head and met his gaze. "Meeks told Francine all about it, and I'm her sister so of course she eventually told me. After that, he swore off love completely and proudly clipped on his playboy badge."

"What crazy fool let him get away? He's gorgeous and rich. She had to be blind, deaf, intoxicated and stupid," he proclaimed. "And not exactly in that order."

Farrah giggled, lifting the image from her mind. "I don't know about all that, but after he found out she was only after his money and was sleeping with someone he thought was a friend at the same time, he ended it and vowed to have no more serious relationships. All he wanted to do was party. And unlike Meeks, he doesn't even care about having an heir. He's leaving all of his money to charity," she said in a wistful tone.

"But—"

"How can you expect me to risk my heart with a man who'll never risk his?" Farrah said, extracting herself from his hold and returning to her chair.

Paul leaned against Farrah's desk and watched as she turned to her computer and began reading over some legal documents.

"Ignore me if you want, but that won't change a thing. That's just one more thing you two have in common, you know—having experienced a broken heart in college. Need I remind you of Jimmy Long and declaring, *I'll never fall in love again*?" he said in a dramatic interpretation of a Southern belle—with a hand over his heart for effect. "After you found out he was only dating you because you fit his family's idea of the perfect mate, someone beautiful from a good family that was on the same social and financial level as them, when all the while he was still seeing his *real* girlfriend from the other side of the tracks."

Yes, Jimmy Long had put up such a really good façade that even her family had fallen for it.

"Whatever happened to him?" Paul asked.

"He married her and I hear they have three kids. His family finally came around, I guess."

"Well, good for them—now back to you."

Farrah turned and gave him a defiant look. "I was twenty at the time. What the hell did I know about love? Anyway, I didn't say I'd never fall in love again. I said I'd never fall *foolishly* in love again. Big difference."

"Is there really any other kind?" Paul asked, frowning down at her.

Farrah ignored his question as she continued, "In fact, I plan to love and get married one day to—"

"To someone weak that you can control and loves you more than you love them," Paul said.

Farrah flinched, but then had to laugh. There was a little truth hidden in those words.

"You'd be bored silly. Safe from heartbreak and no real passion. Not like the out-of-control passion that you feel for Robert. That same passion Francine and Meeks have for each other. Hell, what I feel for John."

Out-of-control is right; if you all only knew just how out of control I'd been. Thoughts of their first night together came to mind.

Robert having her in the private elevator, taking her fast and hard in the living room of their suite before finally gently making love to her until dawn in one of the biggest beds she'd ever seen. The feeling of contentment that engulfed her as she lay in his arms and wanted nothing more than to stay there forever.

Farrah released a wistful sigh and turned back to the documents that required more of her attention than her lack of a love life did at the moment. "Is everything set for New York?"

Paul scowled and picked up his cup. "I can take a hint. Of course everything's all set. Do you think you'll find what you need when you get there?"

"I hope so. We're running out of leads and we've got to find evidence that Ted Jefferson Jr.—or whoever hired Alexia—planted those bogus documents in the first place."

Ted had presented the court with twenty-year-old drawings nearly identical to the ones Robert had developed and filed their patent on. An investigation revealed a set of those same drawings had been buried in the Blake & Montgomery archived records—which presumably had been planted there by their former employee, Alexia. Everyone with system access passed the polygraphs with flying colors.

"How did she even manage to plant the documents in the first place?" Paul asked, frowning.

"That's just it. We haven't been able to figure that out." Farrah slammed her fist against the desk. "We have records of everything in the archived database and while there was a listing for a new system authored by Ted Jefferson during the year in question, the records directed us back to the bogus files we found."

"Wait, those documents are what…at least twenty years old?" he asked, his frown deepening.

"Yeah, and Dad was leading the company then. He knew everything that Ted worked on, and he approved his budget. He's certain that with the technology they were dealing with back then, there's no way Ted could have created anything that Robert could have used to help develop the type of complicated technological designs that he has now."

"So there's no evidence that the system was tampered with?"

"Not that we've been able to find yet." Farrah sat back in her chair.

"What kind of proof will you need exactly?" Paul asked with a deep scowl.

"Mainly, we need to show that Robert's designs were his own and weren't based off anything that anyone else started a million years ago."

"Too bad Senior's no longer in the land of the living. I bet your dad could get the truth out of him. He owes him."

Ignoring Paul, Farrah continued her rant. "And I don't give a damn what Ted Jefferson Jr. thinks. Both he and that traitorous little witch can kiss my—"

Paul sucked in a quick breath. "Calm down, girlfriend."

"It makes me furious that we have to keep defending ourselves over such crap, like we'd stoop to something so low—not to mention hang on to the incriminating evidence. We all know what a brilliant mind Robert has, especially when it comes to computer systems. He doesn't need some old fart's road map to come up with his amazingly innovative design ideas. How dare they try and tarnish his reputation!"

Paul's smiled widened. "Man, you've got it bad...*his* reputation."

"I said *our* reputation." Farrah checked her desktop clock and picked up a set of files that sat in the center of her desk. "I don't have time for this. I have to get over to the law library and check on the Plan B options that Trey and his team sent over."

"Plan B?" Paul asked, his slim lips pulling into a frown.

"In case we can't find a way to prove our innocence."

"Hell, we don't need a Plan B. We're going to find whoever is trying to screw us and put a stop to this madness," Paul stated.

"I agree, but we have to be prepared. We all have a lot of time and money riding on the outcome of this case. Including you, mister. Last time I checked, you had a great deal of stock in the company, too."

"Yeah, well, remember, I already have the best thing that money could never buy—the ability and the *guts* to marry the love of my life." Paul snapped two fingers on his right hand before walking out the door.

Unable to fight back the overwhelming feeling of loss in that moment, Farrah simply whispered, "Something I'll never have…not with Robert, anyway."

Farrah blinked back the sting of tears in her eyes.

Chapter 5

Robert had finally pulled into the garage of his office building after having made several stops to visit clients on his way back. He'd parked his black Porsche 911 Turbo Coupe in his spot, only a few short spaces away from the empty location where its white twin usually held ground, when his cell phone rang. Robert smiled, recognizing the number of the only woman he'd ever really trusted—his foster mother, Penny Hilton—but it faded quickly. He pushed the button to activate his car's Bluetooth.

"Momma Penny, everything all right?" he asked, nervous for her response.

"Of course. You worry about me too much," she said with a small laugh.

Penny Hilton, or Momma Penny as Robert called her, had become Robert's foster mother after his parents died in a boating accident when he was ten years old. The African-American widow had happily taken young Robert in when no other relative had come forward. Momma Penny had been his nanny since the day he was born and later the family's housekeeper when he'd started school. She was his only family and he her only child. They adored each other. Robert's parents' unique approach to child rearing, followed by their sudden deaths, made it difficult for him to connect and trust people. Momma Penny helped him to find some semblance of security.

"Only because you've recently been released from the hospital. Pneumonia is nothing to play with at your age, so take your medicine and follow the doctor's instructions."

"At my age," she huffed.

"You know what I'm saying. How's the new nurse working out?" he asked, hoping she'd let that reference to her growing years slide past.

"He's just fine, although having a male nurse still seems strange to me, you know."

"Yes, I know." Robert grinned, checked his watch and settled into his seat. This conversation was going to take a few minutes and he didn't want to risk losing the connection by leaving the car and going into the building. "But he comes highly recommended."

"So did the last one. What happened to that lovely nurse the agency sent over, anyway? Sonya something. She was very pretty and I liked her. I know she really liked you, too," she said with a smile in her voice that he couldn't miss.

"And that was the problem—she liked me too much," he murmured, more to himself than to his mother. Robert thought back to the night he'd returned home from a late business appointment only to find lovely Nurse Sonya waiting for him at his townhouse. A major problem since she was supposed to be stationed at his mother's place over forty miles away.

"What are you doing here and how the hell did you get in?" Robert demanded as he stood in the doorway of his bedroom.

"I got the address and key from Momma Penny. I waited for your housekeeper to leave and I let myself in," Sonya explained, batting her eyes and playing with her hair. *"Momma Penny's fine. Sound asleep, in fact, so I thought I'd come take care of you. Tuck you in, so to speak."*

Sonya had stolen Momma Penny's copy of the key to his house and evidently had snooped around to find the security code to his system and let herself in. She was waiting in his bed wearing a short and very sexy nurse costume. Had that happened a few years earlier, Robert would have loved playing games with the pretty nurse— even if she had been duplicitous in her attempt to gain his attention—but these days he had no interest in such behavior. He'd fired her on the spot.

Robert knew he'd earned a certain reputation when it came to women. He had fallen in love once, only to have his heart battered and tossed back to him with the gift wrapping still intact. He'd found out that his college sweetheart was only after his money and was sleeping with someone he'd thought was a good friend. A friend whom he'd met as a boy after changing schools when he went to live with Momma Penny. Someone that personally knew Robert's struggles to adjust to the world when his parents died, leaving him with a trust fund and no one, except a woman who wasn't a blood relative, to give him the unconditional love that his parents were unable to provide.

When Robert found out that Momma Penny and not

his mother had been the one to bring him home from the hospital, and had been the one to stay on with the family just to keep his parents from sending him away to boarding school—the same fate relegated to them as children—things began to make sense. His mother and father's hands-off approach to parenting and ultimately their deaths had made it hard for him to trust. So the betrayal of his best friend and his sweetheart had cut deep. Their disloyalty took away the one thing Robert had yet to be able to recapture—his ability to trust his heart to another woman.

Robert promised himself never to enter into another relationship based on anything other than attraction. Lust he could handle; love was a different story. Robert thought that overwhelming feeling and total lack of control were more than anyone should have to deal with. That was, until he'd fallen hard for Farrah Blake. Now the only woman he wanted to be with was her, totally destroying his "bad boy" reputation. Unfortunately, Farrah had seen him at his worst when it came to his appetite for the opposite sex, and now she didn't believe he could ever change. Trying to convince her that he had wouldn't be easy and Robert just hoped that his plan wouldn't backfire.

"What was that?" Momma Penny asked, snapping him back to the present and making him realize she might have overheard something she wasn't meant to.

"Nothing… I need your nurse focusing on you and not me," he said, tightening his grip on the steering wheel.

"Yes, but sweetheart, you really do need someone, a wife to take care of you…to cook for you when I'm gone," she explained.

"First of all, we both know you're not going anywhere," he said, and the thought of losing the older woman sent a piercing pain through his heart. "You promised, remember?"

Every night for three years after his parents died, in order to help him get to sleep at night, Momma Penny would promise she'd never leave him. As he became older, her promise became monthly, then yearly, and had substantially changed to "always being with him even when she wasn't because she'd always be in his heart." Those constant promises had gotten Robert through some very dark days and he'd always be grateful to her for that.

Momma Penny sighed. "Yes, I remember."

"Second, I've been taking care of myself for a long time now. With the exception of our weekly date night, where you insist on cooking for me, I eat quite well on my own. My housekeeper makes and freezes meals for me every week. She ensures that I have plenty to eat," he declared.

"Yeah, most of which you *don't* eat," she scolded.

"And how would you know that?"

"I hired your housekeeper, remember? Besides, nobody can cook like your Momma Penny," she said.

"True," he said, smiling to himself, picturing Momma Penny's look of gratitude after he'd cleared his plate.

"You still need someone special in your life. Preferably a *wife*," she insisted.

"I do need someone and I'm working on it." Robert was surprised at how honest he was being and just how good it felt.

Momma Penny gasped. "Really, who is she?" she asked, her voice filled with excitement, but not letting him answer. "I know she's beautiful since that's the only way you walk…no, wait, it's roll. Which is it, walk or roll?" she asked.

"It's 'roll,' and Momma Penny, please stop watching

all those reality TV shows," he said, chuckling at her new obsession with housewives shows, celebrity dance competitions and anything that started with yelling and ended with fighting.

"When can I meet her?" she pressed. "I only know your male friends. I never get to meet any of your lady friends. They never stick around longer than a few weeks."

"How do you know…? Never mind," he said.

"So, when can I meet her?"

"Soon. I just have to convince her that she needs me, too," Robert promised.

I will convince her, too. Although she's going to be really pissed when she finds out the truth.

"Convince her? Who is this person? She must be crazy. Doesn't she know how lucky she is to have your sights set on her?" she asked, not bothering to keep the shock from her tone.

Robert chuckled at how animated she'd gotten. He could picture her five-foot frame straightening in her favorite chair, where she would be sitting and looking out the big picture window in the living room of the three-bedroom house he'd had built for her several years ago. Momma Penny had always been a lion when it came to her only child, her blue-eyed wonder—the nickname she'd given him as a baby and still used today.

"Momma Penny—"

"You know who I really like?" she asked, that familiar excitement returning to her voice.

Robert sighed, wondering if it was another one of her church members' daughters she was always trying to fix him up with. "Who?" he ventured, but braced himself for the answer.

"One of those pretty, dark-haired girls you work with.

They're sisters. Only I don't know which one is which. That could be a problem…not being able to tell them apart," she concluded.

Oh, I can tell them apart.

"The Blake sisters. And I agree. One would be perfect for me," he murmured, too low for her to hear. The dull ache in his chest that he'd been carrying around for days expanded into something that was spreading through his body like a virus. Last year, Meeks had almost lost his mind when Francine had constantly put herself in danger. And right now, Robert was slowly losing his, because he was in danger of losing the one woman who made him feel alive. The phone fell silent for a moment and Robert knew he'd given himself away. "Wait, how do you even know about the Blake sisters?"

"You're not the only one that can use a computer, you know. Which one is it? Which one's got you all twisted up in the game?" she asked.

"Momma Penny, you're killing me with all this slang," Robert said, laughing.

"I'm waiting," she said, as he heard her take a sip of what he figured was her favorite drink, masala tea.

"Farrah. Her name's Farrah Blake and she's the middle sister…the one with the blue eyes," he explained, inwardly adding, *The color of the deepest part of the ocean.*

"Like my baby boy, although I'm sure yours are much bluer and way nicer, as far as I'm concerned," she stated proudly.

Robert heard a familiar sound entering the garage. He checked his rearview mirror and confirmed his suspicions.

"Momma Penny, I have to go. Take your medicine and I'll call you later," he promised. "And don't give that nurse a hard time, either. Have to keep an eye out for you with these younger men."

"Okay, but you should have thought of that before you hired him," she shot back. "He is kinda cute."

"Momma Penny!"

"Love you, my blue-eyed wonder."

"I love you, too," he replied.

Robert disconnected the call, unplugged his phone and dropped it in his jacket pocket. He exited the car, strolled to where Farrah had parked and was opening her door before she'd barely cut her engine.

"I told you I'd see you later," Robert said, presenting her with a sexy smile. "It's later."

Chapter 6

"What the...? Robert, you scared the hell out of me," Farrah yelled, looking up at him. Her right hand had already reached for the handgun she kept on the side of her seat. "Not to mention you could get shot sneaking up on me like that."

Farrah's dress was pulled up and gathered between her legs. From Robert's vantage point, he had a clear shot of her thighs and legs and she knew he could see that her breasts were rising and falling a lot faster than normal. Farrah could only hope that he thought the adrenaline spike from his sudden appearance was the reason instead of the arousal he always provoked in her whenever he was around.

Robert laughed, as though he found the idea of her shooting him funny. He took Farrah's hand, helped her out of the car, taking her keys in the process and locking her door. Instead of returning her keys, he pocketed them, intertwined their hands and led them toward an area in the garage she recognized immediately. It was a space that was both crazy and special to them both. They would rendezvous there when they wanted to take a few private moments without so many eyes or cameras on them.

"Where are we going?" Farrah asked, only to confirm her suspicions as they passed the bank of elevators leading to their offices.

Robert stopped and pulled her against him, allowing her to feel what she was doing to him. He gazed into her eyes and said, "You know where we're going," before taking her mouth in a kiss that demanded so much more. Robert ran his hand up her back and under her hair. He released her lips, raised her hair and began to kiss and suck gently on her neck. He kissed his way along the edge of her jaw and ran his tongue across her lips before capturing her mouth again. He reluctantly released his hold and pulled her along with him.

"We can't," she said breathlessly.

"Yes, we can." Robert retrieved his security card key from his pants pocket and swiped it in front of a black security box that unlocked the door to a small storage room.

Robert pulled Farrah inside and closed the door. He switched on the light, gently pushed Farrah against the door as he lowered his head and consumed her mouth. Farrah never felt so overwhelmed and out of control as she did whenever she was with Robert. She pressed her body against his and her arms flew up and around his neck. Farrah's fingers buried themselves within his silky, blond-streaked, sandy-brown hair and her hips led Robert's in a synchronized dance that soon had her body screaming for the barriers between them to be removed… quickly.

Robert picked her up and out of her shoes, raising her dress in the process and allowing Farrah to wrap her legs tightly around his waist. With little finesse, Robert unbuttoned and unzipped his pants, freeing himself. With manhood in hand, Robert slid past the lace that covered her core and thrust deep inside of her, but stilled instantly. Farrah's instinct to move was stamped down by Robert's applied weight.

"Damn it," Robert said as he started to pull back.

"What?" Farrah asked on a frustrated gasp, gripping his waist to keep him in place.

"Please tell me you're still on the pill."

"Of course I am," she said, raising her hips and forcing him into a downward thrust.

Robert took Farrah fast and hard, whipping them both into an out-of-control frenzy just the way she liked it. As she felt her body build into what promised to be another amazing orgasm, Farrah moved her hips in a manner that had Robert picking up the pace, ensuring that they would both reach their peak simultaneously. As they both tipped over that blessed cliff, Robert captured the sounds of their release with another mind-blowing kiss.

Robert rested his forehead against hers as they waited for their breathing to return to normal.

"That was—"

"Insane," Farrah supplied on a gasp.

Robert raised his head and gazed into her eyes. "That was incredible, and you are so beautiful."

Farrah felt Robert start to come alive again. "Put me down," she whispered.

Robert extricated himself from her body before he reluctantly obliged her request. Farrah pressed down her dress while Robert adjusted himself back into his pants.

"I can't believe we're here again," Farrah murmured, shaking her head.

"Why? It's perfectly private. You know I'm the only one with a key, and there aren't any cameras here," he explained.

"That's not what I'm talking about and you know it," she snapped, reaching down to pick up her bag. "This is why we have to stay away from each other."

"Why?"

"This can't happen anymore," she said.

Keep it together...keep it together.

"I don't understand why not. We obviously still want each other." Robert took a step toward her, but she threw up her hands to stop him.

"Physical attraction only lasts for so long, and we still have to work together. We can't let any bad feelings that may come from our...from this situation between us," she said, waving a finger back and forth between them, "affect our ability to work together."

"It won't—"

"I know, because we're ending it now before we get in too deep, something neither of us wants," Farrah said, fighting hard to keep the emotion out of her voice. "Once the divorce is final, we can forget this ever happened. Just go back to the way things were."

"You really think that's possible?" he asked.

"Of course. We're adults...not to mention *professionals*. We'll get past this and things will get back to normal. My keys, please," she said, gripping her bag's handle with her left hand, while offering the palm of the other. "After all, we have clients to protect, not to mention a pretty big case to prepare for. Besides, it's just sex that's between us, right?"

Robert looked down at her and offered up a small smile that disturbed her because it didn't quite reach his eyes. "Right, it's just sex," he conceded, placing the keys in her hand.

Farrah gave a wordless nod, turned and walked out the door, leaving Robert standing in the middle of the small storage room.

Who are you kidding? It was far more than just sex... at least to you, anyway.

Farrah made it up to her apartment and into her bathroom, where she quickly removed her clothes. She opened the shower door and stepped under the warm spray, thanking her lucky stars for the automated shower system. Farrah didn't care that it had cost her thousands of dollars. The body jets, the ability to pipe in music, and the fact that the shower turned on at just the right temperature thirty seconds after she pushed a button made it money well spent.

Farrah stood under the oversize showerhead as the water rained down and the side sprays pelted her body. She relaxed into the wonder of wetness for a few moments, when she suddenly felt another presence in the room. Fear was not something that entered her mind. Her nipples tingled; an instant later, moisture pooled between her thighs. Her body knew exactly who the newcomer happened to be.

Farrah smiled and without turning and delivering the scolding that she knew she should, she simply said, "You just going to stand there and watch, or are you going to join me and loofah my back?"

Robert's deep baritone laugh set her body on high alert, anticipating what was to come.

Farrah turned to face him as she continued to wash herself. She watched his utility belt hit the travertine floors, followed by his boots and socks. His shirt was next, then the pants and finally his Calvin Klein underwear. Robert opened the door and joined her under the spray.

"I came by to drop off my copy of your house key," he said, taking the soap out of her hands. "I figured you'd want it back."

"So, instead of waiting for me to get out of the shower, or better still giving it to me later—like at the office or in a couple of days when we leave for New York," she asked, snickering as she enjoyed the sensation of his hands roaming all over her body, "you decided to watch me take a shower?"

"Yeah, that basically sums it up," he said, leaning down to kiss her.

Farrah covered his mouth with her right hand. "It's just sex…an almost-divorced couple just saying goodbye kind of thing. Closure, so to speak…agreed?"

Robert stared into her eyes, and the corner of his mouth curved upward slightly. "Two people finding a little closure tonight. We'd better not waste a second."

Robert kissed Farrah gently on the lips. He used his index finger to raise her head skyward. "Close your eyes, sweetheart. Enjoy the sensation of me and the warm water," he said, kissing the corner of her mouth and down her chin to her neck. He nibbled and licked where her neck and shoulder met, one of her favorite spots. Robert ran his tongue along her collarbone before moving down to the valley of her breasts.

"Hmm…yes…" Farrah caressed his hair and slid her hands down his back.

Robert greedily pulled and teased her nipples as though his life depended on it. He raised his head and stared into her eyes. "You're the most beautiful woman I've ever seen," Robert said softly, his voice cracking slightly.

"I want you," Farrah whispered.

"And you'll have me…all of me," he promised before dropping to his knees. He placed her right leg over his shoulder, gripped her butt with both hands and began kissing and stroking her center. Farrah's head fell back; she seized his shoulders, flexed her muscles to stay upright as she enjoyed the most sensual shower she'd ever experienced. She knew she shouldn't allow this to happen because her heart would pay a heavy price for it, but if this was it for them, Farrah was determined to savor every second.

The next morning, Farrah was so busy reading over several reports regarding Alexia's activities that she didn't even notice when Robert entered her office. Wordlessly, he handed her a large manila envelope.

"What's this?" she asked, putting the pen back in a holder and taking the envelope in her hands.

"It's what you wanted…our divorce papers."

Farrah felt a sharp pain in her heart.

"Oh," Farrah replied, swallowing the lump that had mysteriously lodged in her throat. "So Fletcher got them filed okay," she said, trying to keep her tone as flat as possible.

"Yes. That's your copy." Robert placed his hands in his pockets. "It's been signed by the judge and everything. Now we wait."

"Wait?"

"Yes, thirty days…well, twenty now, and it'll be done. The divorce will be final," he explained nonchalantly.

"Yes, of course," she said, shaking her head.

"So that's it," he added.

"No more Mrs. Gold," Farrah murmured.

"You were never Mrs. Gold…not really," Robert responded.

Farrah fought to keep her emotions under control as she felt tears well in the corners of her eyes. She rushed over to the bar and removed a small bottle of water from the mini-refrigerator.

Farrah casually wiped away a tear before she asked, "Care for something to drink?"

"No, thanks. I have a lot to do before we leave for New York. Hopefully, you're up to speed on all of Alexia's New York escapades, because I'd like to hit up a couple of her old spots when we get there."

Having reined herself in, Farrah spun to face Robert and gave him a wan smile. "Back to business," she said before returning to her desk and taking another swallow of her water. "Of course I'll be ready."

"Good." Robert started to leave.

"Robert, please wait."

He turned and faced Farrah, his features expressionless for the first time she could remember.

"Thanks for being so…discreet regarding this whole situation."

Robert frowned as he stared into her eyes. "Did you think I wouldn't keep my word?"

"No, that's not it at all. I just know it wasn't easy and I…I want you to know how much I appreciate it," she said, breaking eye contact. Farrah picked up the envelope and held it to her chest as though it was a love letter from a long-lost friend, when really it was a world of change that she wasn't quite ready for. She would be more careful. If and when she got married again, it certainly wouldn't be based on losing a bet and allowing friends to goad her into it. And, it seemed, it certainly wouldn't be with Robert Gold.

Robert's eyes dropped to the envelope and his frown deepened. It was obvious that he'd noticed how tightly she held it.

"Well, I might as well put this away," she said, leaving the desk to open the wall safe hidden behind the picture above her bar. She moved a jewelry box to the side and placed the envelope inside. "That's that."

Robert gave her a quick nod and disappeared from her office almost as fast as he had come.

Farrah spent the rest of the afternoon immersed in her work. With the exception of her sisters, she knew it was the one thing that would keep the emotional whirlwind she was currently experiencing in check.

Chapter 7

Robert stood next to Farrah in the living room of an immaculately decorated suite in the Towers of the Waldorf Astoria in New York two days later. The soft blue-and-beige linen sofa with matching wingback chairs and a stone-and-glass-top coffee table with modern, upscale accessories that accentuated the classic colors made for a very romantic setting. The crystal vase filled with a beautiful bouquet of flowers, sitting next to two stemless wineglasses and a crystal bucket holding a bottle of Moscato d'Asti chilling on ice, only enhanced the scene.

Robert could feel Farrah's glare burrowing into the side of his face and he silently cursed his body for responding to her. It had only been a few days since he'd touched her and he still hadn't been able to bring his need for her under control. If anything, his desire was more like a marathon runner getting that second wind to sprint the last few meters to the finish line.

"You did this, didn't you?" she accused through narrowed eyes.

"Did what?" Robert replied, trying and probably failing to sound innocent.

"You know what," she said, placing her hands on her hips. "You intentionally had them place us in the same suite and set up this whole romantic seduction scene, didn't you?"

"No, I didn't," he said, walking over to the flowers and wine to retrieve the card that lay between them. "Shall I read the card?"

Farrah folded her arms under her breasts and gave a quick nod.

Robert opened the card and read it. "Welcome to the Towers at the Waldorf Astoria. Have a drink on us and enjoy your stay. It's signed *Management*." Robert tossed the card back on the table and grinned.

"Fine, what about our accommodations? I *know* Paul didn't make these arrangements."

"Neither did I," he said as he walked over to the fully stocked bar and retrieved a beer from the mini refrigerator, hoping to keep Paul's antics under wraps. If there was one person who was in his corner, it was Paul. Well, actually two if he counted Momma Penny. "Want one?"

"No, thanks," she said, giving him the evil eye.

Robert swallowed down half his beer. "Look, I didn't ask for any of this," he said, using his beer bottle to point around the room. "But it has two bedrooms, so you can have your space and I can have mine."

"With only a living room separating us." Farrah dropped her hands.

"You trying to tell me you won't be able to control yourself or something? Is that what you're saying?" he asked, trying to hold in a smirk because he knew it would infuriate her all the more.

"Absolutely not! I can control myself just fine. Anyway, we'll only be here for a couple of days, if that. As soon as we can find Alexia's contact and chase down who hired her, we're out of here."

"Good." Robert finished off the last of his beer and placed it in the trash.

Farrah remained quiet, and only a simple nod acknowledged her agreement. But her eyes… There was something going on with her eyes that he couldn't quite put his finger on. Was that…sadness he picked up on? What did she have to be sad about? She was getting exactly what she wanted, right?

Robert picked up his suitcase. "I'm going to get a little work done before we have to leave for the play. Will you be ready to go at six?" he asked, staring down into her eyes.

"Six is fine," she said, then quickly turned away from his gaze.

Robert turned and walked into his bedroom and closed the door. He leaned against the door and let out a murmured word that he couldn't quite say in polite company. Robert had witnessed the unshed tears that Farrah was determined to hide from him. He wanted to go to her, confess everything, but he knew she wasn't ready to hear it yet. And since he only had one chance to get it right, he was going to force himself to stay the course or he'd lose her altogether.

Robert walked over to the small desk where he lifted the receiver from the phone's cradle and pressed zero. "This is Robert Gold. Please connect me with Barry Bishop."

"Barry Bishop."

"Bishop? Gold. Thanks for the room upgrade, but how'd you know I was coming?" he asked, leaning against the desk.

"I saw your name on my VIP list and you know I have to make a fellow hotel owner comfortable," he replied, laughing. "You'd never let me live it down if I had you hovering somewhere in the basement."

"Thanks. The flowers and wine were a nice touch."

"Anything for you, Gold. Can we do anything else for you?" he asked, his enthusiasm clear.

"No, thanks. I'll return the favor next time you're in Vegas."

"I'll look forward to it," Barry Bishop replied.

Robert disconnected the call and his cell phone rang. "Yeah, Fletcher, what's up?" he asked, as he moved to the blue, king-size salon bed where he dropped his suitcase.

"Did you give Farrah the divorce papers yet?"

"Yesterday," he replied as he retrieved his shirts and underwear from his suitcase and placed them on the bed.

"And…"

"And nothing. She took them and put them away, just as I suspected she would," he explained.

"She didn't even look at them?" Fletcher asked, surprise evident in his voice.

"No, why would she?" Robert shot back, slipping the shirts in the dresser drawer. "It was uncontested, and now as far as she's concerned, it's finally over…just like she wanted."

"I know, but—"

"No buts. Your part in all of this is done." Robert pulled out his shaving kit.

"What now?" Fletcher asked.

"Now you just keep your mouth shut and I'll take care of the rest. Trust me, I have everything under control."

Sure you do. Robert disconnected the call and headed to the shower.

When Farrah watched Robert retreat to his bedroom, her heart sank and tears stung the back of her eyes, all while her body screamed for attention, the kind of attention that only Robert could supply. "So much for worrying about him crossing the line," she murmured. Farrah hurried past the beautiful flowers, the chilled wine and Robert's tempting door, and right into her bedroom, where she was immediately struck by the room's glamorous décor. The beige walls, glass-faced nightstands, and large crystal chandelier that hovered over gold-and-cream bedding with matching drapery, invoked old Hollywood glamour, reflecting a style similar to her own apartment's.

Farrah placed her overnight bag on the bed and went into the oversize bathroom and smiled. The marble floors, two-headed shower with high-end finishes and Jacuzzi tub big enough for two were too inviting to pass up. Farrah turned on the water and added several of the designer bath beads offered by the hotel. She reached behind her back and stopped. "Why the hell not," she said to her reflection. She returned to the living room and retrieved the bottle of Stella Rosa Moscato d'Asti, uncorked its top and poured herself a glass.

Farrah took several sips as she returned to the bathroom. She placed the bottle and her glass next to the tub, turned off the water and started the jets. She unzipped her dress and let it fall to the tiles. Matching lace bra and panties soon followed and within seconds, Farrah was enjoying that sweet spirited wine and resting her head against the tub's built-in pillow. Between the water and wine, Farrah's eyes drifted shut. She allowed her body to become limp and pliant, letting the water do the work of putting her in a relaxing state. Her mind drifted back several days to when things between her and Robert had "officially" ended.

The memory and pain of Robert's exit jolted Farrah forward, splashing water everywhere. "Get a grip," she admonished herself. "Time to move forward. He clearly has."

Chapter 8

Robert stood in the living room of their suite, wearing a black Armani tux and holding a glass of single malt whisky, admiring the view of Central Park and the East River. He watched the ant-like figures go about their way and brought the glass to his lips when he heard Farrah's bedroom door open. Robert lowered the glass and turned to greet Farrah, only to be caught off-guard at the sight of her. He'd always thought Farrah was beautiful, but the woman standing in front of him, wearing a dark green body-clutching strapless gown with a side split and diamond earrings dangling from lobes exposed by curly, jet-black hair pulled off her face and hanging down her back, was breathtakingly so.

"Well I'm ready," Farrah confirmed, sauntering into the room as she placed her lipstick into her purse. "Are you?" she asked, giving him a lengthy once-over.

Robert slammed back his drink, hoping it would cool

down the fire raging in his blood. He went over to the bar and placed the glass on the marble counter. "Yep, let's go. The car's downstairs."

Farrah grabbed her wrap and headed for the door. They made their way to the bank of elevators and traveled down to the lobby in silence. Soon they were in the limo heading towards the Ambassador Theatre.

"So about earlier…accusing you of messing with the reservation."

His gaze locked on hers.

"I apologize."

"No problem," he replied, sheepishly. "I guess it was kind of my fault."

"What?" Farrah asked, those ruby-red lips pulling into a slight frown.

"One of the owners here is an old friend. He saw my name come across a VIP list, upgraded me, hence *us*, as a courtesy."

"Oh, I understand that," she said, smiling up at him.

"So you think this mysterious person will show up?" Robert asked, trying to keep his eyes on Farrah's face and away from the tops of her beautiful breasts, which were peeking out of her dress.

"Benny assured me that they'll make contact at some point tonight. The only problem is, no one knows exactly what this person looks like," she explained, biting down on her bottom lip, something that only happened when she was a little bit nervous.

"Well, how do you know they'll show up, and how are you supposed to recognize them?"

"Benny's one of my best New York informants and he spread the word that Alexia had a silent partner that's not so silent anymore. He made sure that the right people knew this partner was upset about Alexia's missing client book—"

"What missing client book?"

She gave him an ear-to-ear grin. "Exactly..."

Robert turned in his seat to face Farrah full-on. "What have you done?" he asked in a harsh tone.

"Just took out a little insurance," she said, tossing her hair off her shoulders and crossing one well-toned leg over the other.

"What *kind* of insurance?" he demanded, his protective instinct kicking into high gear.

"I made Benny think there was an appointment book that went missing and that Alexia's partner is really pissed about it. I told Benny to spread the word that her partner has an idea of who took the book and if it's not returned by midnight or some explanation is provided as to what happened to it, all hell would break loose."

Robert's frown deepened. "You made yourself a target?"

"*No*, I made Alexia's non-existent partner a target."

Robert pushed out a breath. "What is it with you Blake women? Always putting yourselves in danger! You have no idea what this guy might do if he thinks you're coming after him."

"That's the point. We need him to be off-guard...to make a mistake. We both know I can take care of myself and you'll be there to back me up. Right?" she asked, giving him a sexy smile.

Robert tried not to be distracted, but his body had other ideas. "I'll always have your back," he said, leaning forward, stopping inches from her face. "No matter what."

Robert saw the gratitude and a glimpse of something

else in Farrah's eyes before she looked away, biting her bottom lip again.

He sat back in the seat, gripping his hands at his sides.

Farrah released a slow breath and sent up a silent thank-you that Robert hadn't seemed to notice just how much his closeness affected her. "Look, all we need is for whoever this person is to show up. I'm sure, between the two of us, we can *convince* him to share whatever information he may have," she declared.

"You think so?"

"Absolutely."

The limo came to a stop in front of the Ambassador Theatre. The line of theatergoers wrapped around the building. The limo door opened and they were ushered past the waiting, nattily dressed crowd into the lobby. The ornate surroundings stopped Farrah in her tracks. The white-and-gold walls showcased expensive mid-century paintings, while the barrel-vaulted and dome ceiling held large crystal and gold chandeliers, and the layers of crown molding spoke to the age of the building. From a time when elegance, glamour and grace were the norm; it was as though they'd been transported into the richness of the past.

"My goodness, this place is beautiful," Farrah gushed with delight as she slowly spun around while keeping her focus on the ceiling's detail. She didn't even notice the people staring or dodging the twirls, trying to prevent collisions.

"Careful, you don't want to get too dizzy," Robert warned, laughing and offering apologetic smiles to those trying to move past her.

Too late, I seem to stay dizzy around you. "No worries, I know my limits." Farrah stopped, beaming up at him.

"Don't I know it," he murmured, and there was a world of meaning in those few words.

Robert walked slowly toward Farrah and stood in front of her before giving her a slow, sexy grin. *He's going to kiss me... I can't let him kiss me...but I want him to.*

Robert leaned forward slightly before he bent down to retrieve the wrap that had fallen to the ground. He straightened, handed it to her and took a step back.

Such an idiot. Thank goodness he's not a mind reader. "Thank you," Farrah said, trying to hide her disappointment.

Robert gave her a tight smile and a slow nod. "So how long is this thing anyway?"

"About two and half hours with a twenty-minute intermission."

"Two hours," he grumbled.

"You'll be fine," she said, eyeing the looks of admiration from a couple of women standing a short distance from where they stood. She couldn't blame them. Robert was a beautiful sight to see in his tux.

A tall, leggy attendant appeared by her side and said, "Excuse me...if you'd please follow me, I'll show you to your seats."

Robert stepped aside. "After you."

Farrah followed behind the attendant to one of four private box seats. The attendant pushed back the thick gold curtain where two plush red velvet seats sat with a small table between them. On the table were two crystal glasses and a silver bucket with a bottle of champagne resting in a bed of ice.

Farrah thanked the attendant before planting herself in one of the seats with the best vantage point.

"This, I'll take credit for," Robert said, retrieving the

champagne bottle. He popped the cork and poured even amounts into both glasses. "So, what now?"

Farrah accepted the offered glass. "Now," she said before taking a sip of the bubbly, "we enjoy the show while we wait. This is Alexia's box, so I'm sure they'll find us. The team's in place?"

"Yeah, everything's covered," he replied, scanning the lower level seating area. "If anyone makes a move toward us, we'll have them in less than thirty seconds."

Farrah settled into the seat and tried to follow her own advice. While she wanted to focus on what was happening onstage, all she could concentrate on was Robert, his profile in particular. The fact that his curly hair hung past his ears just the way she preferred. Those beautiful lips…the things he could do with those lips. And his square masculine chin with a thin film of hair making its presence known was beyond sexy. Farrah's nipples became like mini-marbles and her breathing escalated. She squirmed in her seat as she fanned herself with the playbill.

"You all right?" Robert asked.

"Yes, of course," she said, getting to her feet. "I think I may have taken in that champagne way too fast. I'm just going to the ladies' room."

"The show's about to start. You can't wait until half-time?"

"You mean intermission?" Farrah corrected.

"Whatever…"

Farrah chuckled. "No, I can't. Besides, I know these opening numbers like the back of my hand."

Robert's forehead creased with displeasure.

Farrah almost let go of another laugh, but said, "I'll be right back."

She couldn't get away from Robert fast enough. Farrah made her way down the stairs to the area where the restrooms were. She walked into the ladies' lounge, paused and stared in awe at what lay before her. The room screamed the same old-school glamour as the lobby.

"Wow!" After ensuring she was alone, Farrah did an exaggerated catwalk over to the chaise and flung herself across it. "I need a martini...extra dry," she said, snapping her fingers in the air before bursting into laughter. "I so could have lived large back in the '20s."

The creak of the door echoed and she quickly righted herself.

"I thought you'd never come," said a small, fair-skinned, dark-haired beauty wearing a simple black tea-length dress with silver-sequined tennis shoes.

Chapter 9

"Excuse me?" Farrah said.

The young woman's hand flew to her throat, her mouth open slightly as she took a step back. "Sorry, I just assumed you'd be here at the start of the show like Alexia. She likes to get her business out of the way quickly. Alexia hates missing too much of the first act," she quickly explained.

You're Alexia's associate? You're what, twelve?

"I'm nothing like Alexia," Farrah acknowledged, a little more forcefully than she intended.

"Yes, ma'am. Here you go," she said, quickly offering Farrah a silver flash drive.

The young woman's hand with neon-painted nails was shaking as she placed the drive in the palm of Farrah's hand. *Just go with it.* "Is this everything?" Farrah asked, managing to keep her tone even.

"It's the only thing Alexia gave me. I don't know about anything else…I swear," she said, raising her right hand.

"Have a seat," Farrah said, directing her toward the chair across from her.

"No, thanks, I'm fine," the young woman said, breaking eye contact.

"Do you know what's on it?" Farrah asked.

"I have no idea," she said, shaking her head.

"What's your name?"

"Blige. Blige Summer," she said proudly.

"Well, Blige, I'm Farrah Blake," she said, offering her hand. Blige gave Farrah's hand a quick shake before dropping her hand and taking a step back. "How long *have* you worked for Alexia?" Farrah asked, slipping the drive into her clutch. She tried to remain calm and nonchalant because she knew this could be a critical piece of evidence in finding out who was out to destroy Robert's reputation, their business and why.

Blige frowned, her thin, glossed lips pursed. "Worked for...no, I'm her dependent. I mean, she's my guardian. Alexia is like a sister to me," she explained, shifting a quick look at the door.

Farrah tilted her head. "Her...*dependent*?"

"My parents died when I was eleven. Car accident. Alexia had done some kind of work for them—" Farrah parted her lips, but Blige quickly added, "Don't ask me what, but lucky for me, she felt like she owed them, so she took me in. She's the only family I have. I'd do anything for Alexia."

"I didn't realize," Farrah whispered. "So are you telling me you know nothing about her business?"

"No, ma'am... I mean, yes, that's what I'm saying. She made sure I stayed focused on school," she said, nodding like a bobblehead doll.

"How old are you?"

"Nineteen, but I'll be twenty next month," she said,

raising her chin as if that could make her claim seem more relevant.

Farrah crossed her legs and kept her gaze trained on the wispy teen. She liked the girl's spunk. "Why did *you* have the drive?"

Blige folded her arms, suddenly a little more defensive than Farrah expected. "I didn't steal it, if that's what you think. Alexia gave it to me. She said if for some reason I didn't hear from her in a while or couldn't reach her, just sit tight and someone would contact me with instructions."

Farrah mulled that over for a moment, then said, "When was the last time you talked to Alexia?"

"A few weeks ago, but I wasn't worried," she said shrugging. "She stays so busy. I knew I'd see her over the holidays like always."

"What made you come here tonight? Did someone contact you, tell you to come?"

"Yes and no. Her friend Butch called me and said Alexia had a partner and that you were looking for something and that I needed to be careful." She shifted her weight from one leg to the other. "I figured that was it," she said, pointing at Farrah's purse. "When I saw you sitting in her box, I knew you had to be her partner and that I should probably give you the drive."

"Who's Butch, and what's his last name?"

"It's Johnson. Butch Johnson." Blige bit down on her lip and shifted her eyes downward. "Alexia said he's like her assistant, but I've never met him in person."

"Hmm. Do you…happen to know where he lives?"

"I think she said he lives in New Orleans."

"So how'd you know I'd even be here tonight?"

"I didn't. This is where Alexia always conducts her

business. I'm not sure why, though. So I've been here every night since Butch called me a week ago."

Farrah pushed out a breath. "Sit down, Blige…please."

Blige bit the side of her lip and remained still for a few moments longer before dropping her shoulders and finally taking the seat across from Farrah. She crossed her feet at the ankles and gripped her hands in her lap.

"Alexia's been arrested, and I'm not sure she's getting out anytime soon."

Blige's fair complexion lost all color.

"Did she leave you with any money? Are you going to be able to take care of yourself?"

Blige sat up slightly in the chair and raised her chin again. "Yeah, I'm fine. I have plenty of cash. Alexia even paid for my school in advance."

Farrah checked her watch and realized that Robert was probably wondering about her. "All right, one last thing then, we could be interrupted soon—"

"We won't be," Blige answered. "I paid the attendant to put up the out-of-order sign," she explained. "A little trick Alexia taught me for when I needed privacy."

"Nice trick," Farrah agreed. "Do you have a contact number for Butch?"

"I think I have it in my phone. I'm kinda surprised you don't know him." Blige pulled out a cell, scrolled for a few seconds, and rattled off the information.

Farrah entered the number into her contacts. "We don't have the same circle of friends. Okay, I need you to make me a promise. You can't tell anyone about me or this meeting. It could be very dangerous for you… understand?"

"Okay." Blige lowered her head and sighed. "Do you know how she's doing? Alexia's going to be fine, right?"

Farrah waited for Blige to raise her head and meet her

gaze. "You've been very helpful to me tonight, so I'm not going to lie to you."

Blige nodded, though her teary eyes filled with a sudden flash of anxiety. Farrah got up and took the seat next to Blige.

"Alexia's business required her to do some pretty bad things. She's going to prison for a while. I'm sure she'll contact you when she can. It just may be a little while," Farrah explained, giving her hand a quick squeeze. "But I think she'd want you to go on and make something of your life."

Blige wiped away the tears flowing down her cheeks with shaky hands.

Farrah reached into her purse, pulled out a tissue and handed it to a clearly heartbroken Blige. "We all make choices. You just be sure to make good choices for yourself, Blige," Farrah offered.

Obviously too emotional to speak, the girl simply offered a tight smile.

"You should go," Farrah said, uncrossing her legs and coming to stand in front of Blige.

Blige remained seated, still trying to get her tears under control. "Will you be talking to Alexia soon?"

"I'm sure I will. Why?"

"Do you know if she needs a lawyer? I can help find her one." Blige's voice shook as she spoke.

"I'm sure she has one."

Blige sighed and stood. "Then can you tell her I said… thanks for everything…and that I'm here if she needs me. And that I love her?"

Oh, man.

"I'll make sure she gets the message. I'm sure she'll appreciate it. You just be sure to take care of yourself."

Blige opened her mouth only to close it quickly. She sighed, turned and walked out the door.

"Poor kid. Who would have thought Alexia actually cared about someone other than herself?" Farrah said to her reflection, checking her appearance.

Satisfied, Farrah made her way back to Robert. He had the type of equipment necessary to bypass any security Alexia might have put in place and she couldn't wait to see if they'd struck gold.

Chapter 10

"Looks like we'll soon be headed to New Orleans," Robert said as they entered their hotel suite. "First things first. I'll get Dan's team to try and find out everything they can about this Butch Johnson. They can track him down and sit on him until we decide how we want to approach him."

"Sounds like a plan," Farrah said, removing her earrings. "And I'm not telling you how to do your job, but you should think twice about sending Dell or Cam. They're both young and still pretty green."

Robert raised an eyebrow.

"We are talking about New Orleans," she replied to his obvious confusion. "New Orleans can be a little wilder than Vegas."

"They've been with us for over a year. They know how to handle themselves," Robert assured.

"If you say so. We sure didn't." Farrah dropped her

clutch on the end table, kicked off her shoes and released her hair from its binding. She closed her eyes and combed her fingers through her long locks.

Robert felt a charge whip through his body as he stood in the center of the living room staring at Farrah. His blood raced south and he had to fist his hands at his sides in order to stop himself from taking her into his arms and kissing her senseless—again. "We have to find out what's on that drive before we do anything else," he said in a tone he hardly recognized himself.

"We need to get back and bring everyone up to speed on things. Not to mention I'm dying to find out what's on that flash drive, too. So, are you going to call the pilot about flying us out tonight?" Farrah inquired as she watched Robert flip the drive over in his hand.

"It's nearly midnight, let the man sleep. We'll leave tomorrow as planned." Needing to put a little more distance between them, he walked over to the desk and lifted a room service menu from the tray placed in the center of the desk. "I'm going to order something to eat, you want anything?"

"Sure, anything's fine," she said, heading to her bedroom. "I'm going to go get out of this dress and put on something a little more casual."

Robert felt another charge go through his body. He knew whatever Farrah considered casual would make him very uncomfortable, since her choice of that type of clothing usually consisted of something loose and without a bra. Robert gave Farrah a tight smile and perused the in-room menu; he needed a distraction and also wanted to hide how his body was responding to her. Robert turned at the sound of Farrah's door closing. *You have got to keep it together, man,* Robert admonished himself as he left the menu on the desk and pulled a beer from the mini-refrigerator. The moment he put the bottle to his lips, his phone vibrated. Robert checked the number and smiled. "Hello, beautiful."

"How's my blue-eyed wonder doing?" Momma Penny asked.

"I'm fine. How are you? You're taking your medicine like you're supposed to, right?"

"Yes, sir," she drawled. "You can stop checking up on me. I'm the mother, remember?"

"Yes, ma'am," Robert replied, whipping out the flash drive and placing it inside the briefcase he'd put on the living room table.

"I'm calling to see if I can expect you for lunch tomorrow."

"I'll be there…in fact, can I bring a friend?" Robert asked, bracing for the response.

Even after mentally preparing, Robert still flinched at the sound of Momma Penny's scream.

"Yes, I'm making a pot roast. I know that's a bit heavy for lunch but it's your favorite. I'll just pair it with a nice garden salad and it'll be fine. Please tell me she doesn't have anything against meat. It is a she…right?" Momma Penny inquired and the perplexity in her tone caused him to break out in laughter.

"Yes, Momma Penny…it's a woman. Definitely a woman. And I'm sure whatever you make will be fine," he said, still unable to believe she would even ask such a question.

Momma Penny's sigh of relief was paramount. "All right, Pat and the girls are here. Time for our swim aerobics class."

"Swim aerobics? You sure—"

"Thanks to that heated and covered pool you put in, I

can swim year-round," she said, her voice full of excitement. "I'll see you two tomorrow. Love you."

"Love you, too," Robert said, ending the call before reaching for the hotel phone to place an order.

Farrah walked into her bedroom, slipped off her clothes and dashed to the shower. The lukewarm water that pelted her skin helped to release the tension. Robert was only doing as she'd asked, but the idea that he'd already moved on—according to part of the call she overheard when she came back to retrieve her purse—bothered her more than it should.

She dried herself off, dressed in black leggings and a red oversize shirt that hung off one shoulder. She perched on her bed and wrapped a towel around her damp hair to absorb the moisture, when her iPad signaled an incoming video call.

Farrah hit the connect button and within seconds she was greeted with an image of a fuller, green-eyed version of herself. "Hi, sis, how you feeling?"

"Like a beached whale," Francine grumbled, rubbing her extended belly. "These two refuse to let me get more than a couple of hours' sleep at a time."

"Where's Meeks? Can't he help you with that?" she asked, laughing.

Francine rolled her eyes. "Usually, but I sent him out for dinner."

"Dinner? It's almost eight there, and you usually have your first meal by six. Why are you eating so late, or is this your second helping? You haven't been overdoing it at work, have you?" she asked, glaring at her sister through the screen.

Francine adjusted herself in her chair. "I thought Felicia was the only doctor in the family. Anyway, have you forgotten who my husband is? I'm pregnant with twins, so I'm always hungry. I sent him for tacos," she explained.

Farrah shook her head. "You and those taco cravings."

"It's just another part of our heritage coming through," she proudly proclaimed.

"I guess."

"Never mind my eating habits." Farrah reached for a small pillow and put it behind her back. "So what did you guys find out?"

Farrah spent the next fifteen minutes catching Francine up on everything she'd learned about Alexia, including the flash drive she'd gotten from Blige, and about Blige herself. "So you're telling me Alexia actually cared about someone other than herself?"

"Apparently. You know...we could use Blige to make Alexia talk. We finally found her Achilles' heel."

Francine grimaced. "You want to use an innocent nineteen-year-old girl?"

"No, I want to use Alexia's *feelings* for that nineteen-year-old innocent girl," she clarified, unwrapping the towel to pull her hair up into a high ponytail. Then she zeroed in on something amazing. "Did...did your stomach just move?"

"Yes, it does that," she said, rubbing her abdomen with the palms of her hands. "So—"

"Why?" Farrah asked.

"There are two babies in here trying to get comfortable," she explained. "Just like I am."

"Is that weird...? Does it hurt?"

Francine laughed. "It's uncomfortable at times, but it's wonderful, too."

"If you say so," Farrah mumbled, clearly not sure she would agree with her sister.

"So what's next?"

"We'll be home sometime tomorrow afternoon," Farrah replied, reaching for her lotion and hairbrush. "Robert wants to use his system to open the drive. He thinks there will be encryption software that he'll have to break."

"All right, I hear Meeks coming," Francine said, giving her belly a few gentle pats. "Time to feed these babies, not to mention their mother."

"Enjoy." Farrah leaned closer to the screen, crooning, "Bye, babies, Auntie loves you so much. Seriously, sis, you two really need to give those kids some names."

"We're working on it," Francine quipped before blowing a kiss and signing off.

Before Farrah could close the iPad, another signal came through, requesting an open line for a video conference. *What now, Francine?* A wide smile crawled across Farrah's face when a clean-faced, sloppy-ponytail-wearing, hazel-eyed version of herself popped on the screen. "Well, hey, sis, isn't this a nice surprise. Is everything okay? I thought we weren't going to talk about the baby shower again until next week."

Felicia, the youngest of the Blake triplets, smiled. "Everything's fine and I didn't call about Francine's baby shower. But now that you've mentioned it, how are you coming with your search for a location?"

"Well, I've been busy working with Trey on the appeal…" Farrah stopped speaking when she saw her sister knit her brow. "What?"

"You haven't done a thing since we talked about this last week, have you?" she asked, leveling an accusatory glare at her sister.

"Look, sis," Farrah said, raising her hands in surrender. "We've been knee-deep in it around here. Besides, we have plenty of time."

"Not." Felicia raised her index finger and turned to address a small Asian woman who handed her a clipboard to review. She quickly scanned the documents, then she fluently exchanged a few words in Korean before signing the papers and turning back to her sister. "Where was I?"

"I hate that you know a language that I don't," Farrah said, poking out her lip like an angry child would when they couldn't get their way.

"Because Spanish and French aren't enough for you. You're just nosey," Felicia shot back.

Both sisters laughed.

"Back to the subject at hand. We don't have enough time if you want to stick to that winter wonderland theme and have it in December," Felicia said. "You know how fast things get booked up, and I don't care how much power or money we have, we're not bumping another party because you didn't make a call or refuse to delegate."

"First of all, that only happened once and that couple was more than happy to move their wedding date."

"Only after you offered to pay for their wedding," she reminded Farrah.

Farrah shrugged. "So it was worth it. The Houston Club is where John proposed to Paul. The wedding *had* to be there."

"Anyway…"

Farrah sighed. "All right, I'll ask Paul to look into some locations and if we have to move it to January, so be it. Happy now?"

"Yes. And I'm going to follow up with Paul and make sure you're on top of things, too." Felicia picked up her bowl and took a bite of something unfamiliar.

"What are you eating?"

"Fish and rice."

"For breakfast?" Farrah scowled.

"I'm on the other side of the world, remember? It's late *afternoon*. This is my lunch," she explained. "And it's soooo good."

"So if you didn't call about the shower, what's so important that it pulled you away from finding a cure for erectile dysfunction for members of the CIA?"

Felicia covered her mouth to keep from spraying her food as she laughed. "Erectile dysfunction, really? We've talked about this already, and while I *still* can't tell you what I'm working on, I assure you that I'm not having anything to do with the male anatomy. Directly or indirectly."

"Oh, yeah, I forgot, you're holding out for Mr. Right."

"Why must you always go there? No, I'm doing my job," Felicia shot back, taking another bite of her food. "Now can we please get to the real reason why I called?"

"What's up?" Farrah asked as she began to spread lotion down her arms.

"You know how I'm having Paul handle my mail?"

"And…"

"Well, I received something that came to me through the Chicago office." Felicia held up a white envelope.

"It was sent to you through the CIA mail? What is it?" she asked.

"A letter from a law office out of Atlanta, an S. Peters. Have you ever heard of him or the firm McCormick and Associates?"

"It doesn't ring any bells."

"Do you remember my college roommate Valarie Washington?" Felicia asked. "Well, it's Valarie Washington-Sawyer now, actually."

Farrah thought for a moment, then nodded slowly. "She had cancer, right?"

"Yes. Well, she died recently and named me as sole heir to her estate."

"What!"

"I know," Felicia said, sighing, and her brow puckered. "The letter states that I have to appear in person to stake my claim and hear the terms of the will. The sooner, the better."

"That's going to be a little hard, considering you're on the other side of the world."

"Tell me about it. But we'll be wrapping things up here in a couple of weeks, so I can stop in Atlanta on my way home. So can you check them out for me?"

"Me? Really?" Farrah teased. "You mean, you don't want to get one of your CIA buddies to handle it for you?"

"Now why would I want to do that when my sister is a brilliant lawyer—who graduated at the top of her class and kicks butt on a regular basis—and handles things like this every day?"

Farrah looked amused. "Pouring it on a little thick, aren't we?"

"I'm sure it'll end up being something you'll be handling for me sooner or later anyway."

"True," Farrah said, grinning and fanning herself. "No problem. I'll see what I can find out, so just scan me the letter."

"Thanks, sis."

"Anytime."

"I better go. I know it's late there, so we'll talk soon. Sleep well." Felicia sent her sister an air kiss and ended the call.

"With Robert nearby, that's not likely," she said to the blank screen.

Chapter 11

Farrah returned to the living room to find a table set with several silver dome-covered dishes. The wonderful aromas assaulted her senses. Unable to help herself, she lifted the first set of covers. Her breath caught at the sight of each dish: shrimp cocktail, steak sliders, hot wings, French fries and chocolate cake—all of her favorite foods. "He remembered," she murmured, fighting the emotions that sprang forward.

"Of course I did," Robert said, his low vocal register and fresh scent snatching her attention. "I remember every single detail about our time together."

Farrah turned and the sight of Robert stole her breath. He had changed into a pair of low-riding jeans and a white V-neck T-shirt with several silky hairs from his chest peeking out. He was barefoot and leaning against the doorjamb with his hands in his pockets—his face nearly expressionless.

Farrah gave her head a small shake before she spoke. "Thank you…everything looks wonderful," she said, turning back to the feast.

"Wait," Robert ordered, walking up behind her, putting only a few inches between them. "I never told you what a great job you did today. And you looked beautiful doing it, too."

Robert's large frame and intoxicating scent wrapped around Farrah like a comfortable blanket. Farrah leaned into him at first, and his hands stroked her arms, causing a shock of desire to whip through her body. Suddenly she gripped the table, bringing herself under control. "Thanks," she whispered.

Farrah felt the immediate sense of loss when he took several steps back. "Want a beer?" Robert asked.

"Sure."

Robert smiled, handed her a beer and took a seat at the table. "Let's eat," he said.

Farrah took the seat across from Robert and studied her selections. "So when we—"

"No," Robert said, waving his hand in front of his face. "No more business. Not tonight."

"Well, we're certainly not talking about our ill-fated relationship." Farrah placed two steak sliders on her plate. "So what should we talk about?"

Robert added two sliders to the wings he'd already plated. "How about we discuss your latest moves in our Fantasy League?"

"What about them?" Farrah asked with a slider halfway to her mouth.

"You benched a world-class defensive end so a mediocre running back could play."

"Says you… That mediocre running back is starting

this week. I have a good feeling about him." Farrah took a bite of her sandwich.

"Well, enjoy that feeling. That's about the only real pleasure you'll be getting from that experience." Robert held Farrah's gaze as he, too, took a bite of his sandwich.

In spite of their differing opinion on the recent NFL trades and the fact that Farrah was kicking Robert's butt in their Fantasy Football League, they had a relaxing evening just like a real couple.

When that realization hit, Farrah admonished herself for such thoughts. *Get it together, girl. This distant, business-only, platonic relationship is what you wanted. Deal with it.*

Robert spent the night fighting his desire for Farrah. He'd nearly lost all control when Farrah had leaned back into him, especially with her soft shoulders and erect nipples calling to him. Robert found the will to step away after he noticed how white Farrah's knuckles had become as she gripped the table. Seeing how his nearness affected her, too, reinforced his resolve. He had to lose a few battles if he wanted to win the war. The constant arousal he felt when she was near was getting to him, but Farrah was worth the discomfort.

It was a little before noon when they landed at Houston's Hobby Airport. They made their way through the VIP terminal for private jet owners to his waiting car.

"Thanks, Jimmy," Robert said to the stocky valet who started loading their bags into the trunk of a black Mercedes.

"Where's the Porsche?" Farrah asked, rifling her bag for her Chanel sunglasses.

"I had Jeremy bring the sedan and take the Porsche back to my place. I knew we'd need the room."

"Oh," Farrah said, giving him the side-eye.

"For the luggage," he clarified.

Farrah grimaced as she slipped on the sunglasses.

"My mother's expecting us for lunch. I hope you don't mind."

"Your mother?" she asked, returning her eyeglass case to her bag. "And what do you mean *us*?"

"The woman who raised me," he clarified.

"You mean your foster mother."

"I don't call her that. We're closer than that. She called last night while you were in the shower to remind me of our standing date," he explained as he held the door open for her.

Farrah stared up at him and frowned. "Your mother called…about lunch…when I left to take a shower?"

Robert could see that something he'd said confused her but he couldn't figure out what it could be. "Yes."

"To remind you of your lunch date," she repeated.

"Yes," he replied. "So, will you join me?"

Farrah bit down on her bottom lip as she looked down at her outfit—black jeans, a simple red V-neck shirt and matching black jean jacket. Robert could see indecision flash in her eyes and quickly added, "You look great, and it's just lunch. No big deal. Momma Penny has wanted to meet the Blake sisters for a while now."

Farrah released her lip and shrugged. "Sure, why not. Like you said, it's just lunch," she conceded, sliding into the passenger seat.

Robert closed the door and made his way to the driver's side, trying not to smile. He slipped behind the wheel, pulled out of the drive and into slow-moving traffic.

"So where does your foster mother live?"

"About twenty miles outside of downtown," he replied, referencing the area as he turned off the highway, heading toward the freeway. He moved to the far lane where he tested the boundaries of the city's speed limit.

"You don't talk about her or your childhood…ever. The only way I knew you even had family was because Meeks told Francine. Why don't you ever talk about her?"

"No reason. I just don't share my private life with many people. Momma Penny is a big part of my life. She's all the family I have and she's pretty special to me."

"That's great. So, no one's ever met her before… I mean other than Meeks and your college buddies, right? I remember hearing a few of those stories," she asked, her eyebrows raised slightly.

Without taking his eyes off the road, he said, "What are you asking me, Farrah?"

"Fine." Farrah turned her body toward Robert and crossed her arms under her breasts. "How many of *your* women has she met?"

Robert gripped the steering wheel, but remained silent as he checked his rearview mirror before exiting the freeway. He pulled into a popular grocery store parking lot, parked and cut the engine. Robert took a deep breath and pushed it out slowly before he turned and met her gaze. Farrah continued to glare at him—clearly waiting for an answer. If he wanted her to understand him better and trust that it was possible for him to love and commit himself to someone—to her—he had to open up and share more of himself.

"Penny Hilton, or Momma Penny, as I'd come to call her, was my nanny from the day I was born. In fact, there are photos of her carrying me out of the hospital instead of my parents," he explained.

Farrah remained silent, her face devoid of expression.

"My parents were very busy people," he started to explain. "My father was a corporate attorney and my mother was a socialite. I was their only child and they loved me…in their own way. They just didn't have time for me."

Farrah's shoulders dropped; she clasped her hands in her lap but remained silent.

"They died in a boating accident when I was ten."

"I'm sorry. I had no idea you were so young when you lost your parents. That must have been devastating," she said, reaching over and squeezing his forearm.

"It was hard, but not for the reason you think."

Farrah's forehead furrowed and she dropped her hand. "What do you mean?"

"I mean, I loved my parents, but I didn't know them. I hardly saw them." Robert's brows puckered as several painful memories flashed through his mind. "I had nannies seven days a week and if not for Momma Penny, I would've been shipped off to boarding school on my fifth birthday."

Farrah's frown deepened. "Fifth…seriously?"

"Both my parents were only children from wealthy families and that's the way they were raised," he said nonchalantly. "My grandparents shipped them off when they were about that age."

"So how did she stop them?"

"Momma Penny basically agreed to raise me full-time. She took me home on the weekends and agreed to handle anything school-related—from parent-teacher conferences to all social and athletic activities."

"Unbelievable…"

"Momma Penny didn't mind." The corner of Robert's mouth rose slightly. "By the time I was five, she was widowed in her midthirties, and she'd never had any children of her own. So she thought of me as her second chance. In reality, she was my only chance. My only chance at a real life, anyway, a happy childhood. And she gave me every bit of that."

Farrah swiped away a single tear.

"So after my parents died, she kept me."

"You didn't have any other family that wanted you?"

The slight smile disappeared. "There were a couple of great-aunts and uncles that came forward but after they found out they wouldn't have access to the money my parents left me—other than the small monthly allowance set aside to help with my expenses—they all walked away, and I became a ward of the state."

"Until Momma Penny stepped in, that is," she confirmed.

"Yep, and she never cared about the money. Not even the monthly allowance she was entitled to, but she had no choice. Momma Penny refused to leave me at the mercy of the state and she didn't want to have to work so much that she couldn't raise me right. She made sure we had a good life but more important, that we were always together." Robert smiled at the memory.

"Wow, she really loves you."

"She does. And I love her, too…very much. So to answer your question, no, I haven't brought any women to meet Momma Penny. No one's been special enough to me. Until now…until you." Robert leaned over and ran the back of his hand down the side of her face as he stared at her lush mouth.

"Oh…" she gasped, and Robert dropped his hand, faced forward and quickly started the car. He had to get moving before he pulled Farrah onto his lap, kissed her breathless and confessed everything. "Ready?" he asked.

"Yes, I think I'm getting there," Farrah whispered.

For some reason Robert didn't think she was just talking about a visit to his mother.

Chapter 12

Farrah watched as they made their way through an upscale neighborhood designed for senior residents fifty-five and older, keeping her focus on the changing landscape. While she was still reeling from all she'd learned about Robert in the last twenty minutes, Farrah took notice of a French country house with a wide wrap-around porch, with two large trees and a bed of roses that were so beautiful they didn't look real.

"Here we are," Robert said as he exited the car.

He quickly made his way around and opened Farrah's door. She gifted him with a wide smile and accepted the hand he offered. "Wow, this place is beautiful."

"I designed and had it built a couple of·years ago," he said proudly. "It was her Mother's Day gift."

Farrah opened her mouth to speak but before she could get her words out, the front door opened, which was followed by a high-pitched scream.

"There's my blue-eyed wonder," an elegantly beautiful caramel-skinned woman called, standing on the porch. She wore a floor-length, short-sleeve flowered dress, and her long, salt-and-pepper hair had been plaited in a braid that hung across her shoulder. Her skin was practically wrinkle-free and she looked nowhere near her sixty-plus years. *Robert was right; his mother is beautiful.*

Robert smiled as he hurried up the wooden stairs and onto the huge porch. "Momma Penny," he said, reaching down to embrace and kiss her while simultaneously lifting her and spinning with her in his arms.

The sight made Farrah's heart expand even more for the man she was trying to release. The love between the two was obvious. The petite woman, who looked barely five feet tall and no more than a hundred pounds, was playfully hitting Robert while demanding that he put her down.

Robert complied and reached for Farrah's hand. "Momma Penny, I'd like you to meet a *special* friend of mine." Robert intertwined their fingers and guided her forward. "This beautiful creature is Ms. Farrah Blake."

"Well, finally! I'm pleased to meet you," she said, offering her well-manicured hand while giving her an interested once-over.

"It's a pleasure to meet you, too, Mrs. Hilton," Farrah replied, taking in the woman's dark brown eyes and pleasant smile.

"Child, I haven't been Mrs. Anybody in a very long time. Call me Momma Penny," she insisted, giving Farrah's hand a small shake. "Let's get inside out of all this heat. It may be late October, but it's still hot as Hades out here. I just made some sweet tea, so let's go have some, shall we?"

Farrah and Robert followed her into the immaculately

decorated house. To Farrah, it felt more like walking into a French painting. The cream walls, coffered ceiling and mahogany floors that ran throughout the house were a perfect setting to the rich green, cream and gold furnishings. The view offered beyond the wall of French doors to the enclosed pool was nothing short of breathtaking.

"Please have a seat," Momma Penny instructed, directing them to a sofa. "Lunch will be ready shortly."

Robert settled into the spot next to Farrah with his arms stretched across the back of the sofa and his right foot resting on his left knee, while Momma Penny took a seat in one of two circular chairs facing them. Farrah was completely taken by the simple elegance of her surroundings.

"Momma Penny, your home is lovely, simply beautiful." Her attention was immediately drawn to the white baby grand that sat in the corner across from the oversize picture window that faced the front of the house. "Oh, my, what a beautiful piano. Do you play?"

"Oh, heavens, no, my Robert plays," she said, beaming proudly at him. "I guess he's never played for you."

Farrah gave Robert a sideways glance. "No, he most certainly has *not* played anything for me."

"The opportunity has never presented itself," he defended, shifting so that both feet were firmly planted on the wooden floor.

"There's no time like the present," Farrah teased, stroking a hand over his.

Momma Penny smiled.

"Maybe later. Momma Penny, didn't you say something about sweet tea?" Robert got to his feet. "I'll make a glass for everyone."

The women laughed as he quickly retreated to the kitchen. "Check on my bread while you're in there,"

Momma Penny called after him. "It should be time to come out of the oven."

"Yes, ma'am."

Momma Penny reached out to the square wooden coffee table in front of her chair, pulled open one of the two drawers attached and retrieved a large photo album. She joined Farrah on the sofa. "I thought you'd like to see my Robert when he was just a little something."

Farrah eyes widened. "I'd love to see that."

"Before I show you my baby's pictures," she said, keeping her hand on the leather embossed album cover, "I want you to know what a wonderful man my son is."

Farrah smiled. "Really? And you wouldn't be a little biased, Momma Penny?"

"Well, maybe a little," she said with a little chuckle. "Oh, he pretends to be all hard—and I know he's tough—but in reality he has a soft heart when it comes to women."

Farrah gave the woman a knowing glance. "Soft heart?"

Momma Penny gave Farrah's hand a gentle pat. "I know he used to date a lot—thank goodness he's done with that phase of his life—but when he finally finds *the one*, I know things will be different."

"I don't know," Farrah said, shaking her head. "I mean, he was in love once, and that didn't work out."

"Child, that wasn't love." Momma Penny dismissed the thought with a nonchalant wave. "That was college lust and wounded pride. That little girl was only after my boy's money. In my day we called girls like that gold diggers."

"We *still* call them that," Farrah offered.

"I told him to watch out, but when you're dealing with young hormones, it's a waste of time. You just pray they come to their senses. Which he did," Momma Penny declared.

"No disrespect, but I think it messed him up a bit."

"No, it just allowed him to sow some wild oats, so when the right one came along, he'd be ready," she explained, stroking the photo album's cover. "And believe me, he's ready."

Farrah laughed. "You sure about that?"

"Of course. Why do you think you're the only woman I've ever met? I'm pretty special in his eyes, you know. His words, not mine."

"Yes, ma'am, I can see that."

"Which makes you pretty special yourself." Momma Penny patted her hand. "Now, you ready to see my blue-eyed angel when he was a baby?"

"Absolutely," Farrah said, rubbing her hands together with glee.

Robert heard the laughter coming from the living room, which could only mean one thing. He picked up the three glasses of tea with both hands and made his way back. He paused when he saw Farrah and Momma Penny sitting with their heads together, poring over a photo album he recognized immediately.

Farrah looked up and a wicked smile spread across her face. Robert's head tilted slightly and returned her smile. *Damn, she's beautiful.*

"So your mother has been showing me some of your baby pictures. Robert…" Farrah waved her hand in front of her, making a half circle "…the early years," she added, giving him a quick wink.

Momma Penny laughed with both hands covering her mouth.

"Momma Penny, you promised," he chided, handing them each a glass before taking a chair across from them.

"What?" she said, placing a single hand on her chest, making an attempt to seem innocent.

Farrah took a swallow of her tea. "This tea is wonderful."

"Thank you, dear, it's my special recipe," she stated, then pointed to one image in particular. "Oh, here's my favorite. He was about twelve when my sister took this. Robert was so proud of how he was able to help me braid my hair." She held a picture of a young Robert standing behind the chair where Momma Penny was seated. He had a long, dark braid in his hands.

Robert nearly choked on his tea. "Momma Penny…"

Farrah looked at the picture. "Wow…he actually braided your hair. Hmm…"

"He sure did. He still helps me from time to time," she proclaimed, squeezing Farrah's forearm. "Oh, let me go check on my roast. I'll be right back, and then I'll show you the high school albums. He played every sport you can imagine and I have the pictures to prove it."

"I can't wait," Farrah said on a laugh as she watched Robert's frown deepen.

"So, how old were you when you went through this naked chubby stage?" she asked, waving a picture of a young Robert wearing nothing but cowboy boots, a cowboy hat and a plastic toy gun belt strapped to his small hips.

Robert lowered his head and shook it slowly.

"At least it's only the back of you," she said, giggling.

"You're really enjoying this, aren't you?" he shot back, sliding over to take the album from her. *Enough of this.*

"Yes… I truly am," Farrah said, laughing, leaning back on the sofa.

"Lunch is ready," Momma Penny called from the kitchen.

"Thank goodness," Robert said, relieved at having an immediate reprieve. "Shall we?" Robert offered Farrah his arm and escorted her into the kitchen.

"A hair-braiding, piano-playing athlete. Who would have thought?" Farrah said. "I can't imagine what else I don't know about you."

"Soon you'll know absolutely everything, I promise," he whispered in her ear before gently kissing her on the cheek.

Chapter 13

Robert had just sat down at his extra-wide mahogany wood desk, powering up his computer and adjusting his double monitors—still overwhelmed by the instant closeness between Farrah and Momma Penny—when Meeks walked into his office. Meeks held his cell phone and iPad in one hand while he clipped the keys to his utility belt with the other.

"Sorry I'm late. So what's on it?" Meeks took a seat in front of Robert's desk, placing his iPad on its corner and his cell in his pocket.

"What's on what?" Robert asked, sliding in his chair over to the extra-long wood-and-stainless-steel-top credenza that took up nearly an entire wall, where he turned on two additional computers.

"The flash drive," Meeks said.

"I don't know. I haven't opened it yet." Robert returned to his desk. "I just got in."

"You just got here?" he asked, checking his watch. "What happened? Your plane landed three hours ago."

"We had lunch with Momma Penny, and you know how that goes."

Meeks smiled and nodded. "I sure do. How is… Wait, we? Who is we?" he asked, his eyebrows coming to attention.

"Farrah."

"You took Farrah to meet Momma Penny?" he asked in a slow drawl, as if he was trying to figure out what such an action could mean in his own mind.

"It was lunchtime when we landed, so I took her out to eat. It just so happened to be at Momma Penny's house." Robert turned back to his computer and inserted the drive.

"Bull!" Meeks shot back. "You don't have personal interactions of any kind when it comes to women. Hell, everyone knows you don't even let women come to your house. You certainly wouldn't take just *anyone* to meet Momma Penny, even if you were in the neighborhood. So, what's up?"

"Nothing, it was just lunch…and Farrah's not just anyone." Robert continued examining the messages popping up on his screen. "Just as I figured, there are multiple levels of security and firewalls in place. Alexia is good. But I'm better."

"How long?"

"Ten…fifteen minutes tops," Robert replied.

"Good, that gives us plenty of time," Meeks said, leaving the seat and retrieving two bottles of water from the mini-fridge.

"Time for what?"

Meeks placed one in front of Robert before he cracked the seal of his own bottle. He took two big swallows and returned to his seat. "Time for you to tell me what's really going on between you and Farrah."

Robert's hand stilled over the computer's keys for a moment before entering the code necessary to start his decryption program. He hit a final key, stood and looked out his window while Meeks sat in silence. There were very few people Robert trusted. He could trust Meeks with anything. Meeks was like the brother Robert never had and always wanted, but he wondered just how much truth Meeks was ready for. He took a deep breath and turned to face his friend. "I'm in love with Farrah," he confessed.

"Tell me something I don't already know."

"How much you want?" Robert asked, gripping the back of his chair.

Meeks's gaze darted from Robert's hands and back up to his face. "That bad?"

"How much?"

"Will I have to keep it from Francine?" Meeks asked.

"For a while anyway," Robert confirmed. "We both know how hard it is for you to keep anything from your wife."

"All right, then, give me enough to convince me that you're both okay and that Farrah won't get hurt," Meeks said.

"Fine." Robert sat back down. "I'm trying to convince her that I'm not the commitment-shy playboy she thinks I am."

"Hmm."

"Not anymore, anyway," Robert added, raising his right hand as though he was being sworn in and about to give a testimony. "I'm hoping that once she sees there's more to me than what she thinks she knows, she won't be afraid of what she's feeling and be willing to give us a chance."

"And introducing her to Momma Penny was a start?" Meeks inquired.

"Yep."

Meeks offered a slow nod, rubbing his chin with the thumb and index finger of his right hand. "All right, so you think she has strong feelings for you, too…beyond the obvious."

"The obvious?" Robert asked.

"As you once told me, a blind man can see how much you two are attracted to each other."

"Yeah, well, it's more than that…much more."

Meeks took another swig from his bottle. "You're so private about everything. You don't let people get too close."

"I know, and I'm working on it," Robert admitted.

"When did you come to this realization?"

"A few months ago, but I think things have been building for a while now. I just wasn't sure how to pursue it." Robert looked away briefly, trying not to show Meeks more than he was prepared to explain. "But an opportunity presented itself and I went for it."

"An opportunity…?" Meeks asked, scratching his chin.

"Yes. And that's when things got…complicated," Robert confirmed.

"I bet. You know your reputation is going to be hard to live down."

Robert slammed his fist against his desk. "Damn it! That was years ago."

"Yeah, to you and me," Meeks countered. "To women, you can be sixty and they'll still be looking at you sideways when it comes to other women."

Robert's shoulders dropped. "Francine didn't have

a problem with your past. And we both know you had your fair share of dirt. Need I remind you… Jasmine?"

"How could I forget? She nearly destroyed my life."

Jasmine Black, a beautiful thirty-year-old redheaded Italian-American, was an ambitious security specialist and Meeks Montgomery's former lover, who'd become obsessed with Meeks and tried to kill Francine to get her out of the picture.

"Besides, Francine and I had other issues to work through." Meeks grimaced; clearly memories of that experience were still hard to handle. "Look, I wish you luck. Just remember their father raised all three of his beautiful girls to be brilliant, independent and tough as nails. Those Blake women aren't to be played with."

"Tell me about it," he said, grinning at the familiar warning. Robert's computer beeped. "Twelve minutes. Damn, I'm good." Robert stared at the multiple file names that appeared on the screen.

"So, what's it say?" Meeks asked, leaning forward in his chair.

"There are a lot of files here," Robert responded, clicking a few keys to navigate through the maze of folders. "Looks like individual client files with notes and attachments, pictures I'm sure. There's a calendar, something that appears to be a client list, and tons of surveillance documents."

Meeks got up and came around the desk and stood next to his friend as he stared down at the cursor waiting to be hit. "Alexia was very organized," Meeks confirmed. "Open the Blake & Montgomery file."

Robert browsed through the contents until he came across a set of documents that stopped both men in their tracks—a scanned copy of earlier versions of several drawings and outlines for security systems that Robert and Meeks had worked on within the past five years. "You need to call Farrah and Francine. Get them in here."

Meeks didn't move. He continued to stare at the screen.

Robert fought through his own anger, stood and faced his friend. "We're going to find whoever stole our material, find the forger and clear our name. I'll call Paul and have him track down Farrah and Francine. They need to see this, too," he said, reaching for the phone on his desk.

Meeks gave a short nod. "Whoever's behind all this has to be close. They were able to plant someone in our organization that could not only steal confidential information, but managed to plant bogus documents that forced us into this mess. We could lose millions. Not to mention the hit our reputation will take," Meeks said.

"Being labeled a liar and a thief doesn't bode well in our field. We'll find whoever's behind this and we'll make them pay," Robert promised.

Chapter 14

"What's so important that Paul had to pull me out of a meeting? Whatever it is couldn't have waited?" Farrah chastised as she walked into Robert's office.

The sight of Meeks's stiff spine as he looked out of the window and Robert's strained expression from his spot behind his desk told Farrah something was wrong. "What's happened? Is Francine okay?"

"I'm fine," a familiar voice called from behind her.

At the sound, Meeks's shoulders dropped and he rushed to Francine's side. He took her hand and guided her to the chair that he'd long abandoned. The look of love in his eyes made Farrah's heart ache, and she quickly trained her sights on Robert, who'd seen it, too. She tamped down on the instant feeling of longing that flashed through her. "What's going on?" she demanded, crossing the few feet to stand in front of Robert's desk.

"Robert cracked Alexia's security," Meeks explained

as he stood holding Francine's hand. "We thought you should see what we found."

"It must not be good by the look on your faces," Francine said, looking first to her husband, then to Robert.

"It's…unexpected," Meeks said, his face devoid of its normal expression.

"Well, don't keep us waiting," Farrah commanded. "Let's see it. What's got your back up?"

Robert cut his eyes to Meeks, who gave him a small nod. "The folders contained a number of different files, a calendar of events, financial records, and surveillance photos."

"Surveillance photos?" the sisters asked simultaneously.

"Alexia was keeping tabs on people. Their comings and goings…and there're photos," Robert explained, placing his hands in his pockets. "It dates back six months before she first made contact with Farrah."

"That's not so unexpected. Why are you looking like someone just told you superheroes never existed?" Francine asked no one in particular, but kept her focus between Robert and Meeks.

"Because they don't," Robert and Meeks chorused.

"Do, too," both sisters replied, glaring at the men.

Meeks smiled and squeezed Francine's hand. Farrah knew teasing was his way of keeping Francine calm, reassuring her that everything was going to be fine. "What is it?" Farrah asked.

Meeks looked over at Robert, who had come from around his desk to stand next to Farrah. Robert took Farrah's hand and intertwined their fingers, instantly gaining her mind and body's attention. "She had your picture."

"That's not a surprise," she said with a scowl. "I was her target. I'm the one who hired her. She had to find a way to get information about me. Otherwise, she wouldn't have been able to nail her interview the way she did."

"And?" Francine asked, knowing there had to be more.

"Alexia gained access to a lot more confidential material than we realized. Material that's kept under lock and key…and under *your* supervision," Meeks explained to Farrah.

"But how could she have gotten past our security system? You all know how I am about my safety measures in place. She must've somehow got ahold of the *multiple* combinations to my safe to get all the override system security codes. Do you know how hard that is?"

"Yet somehow she did," Meeks said. His voice held a note of skepticism.

Farrah's eyes cut to Robert, who was gripping her hand a little tighter, offering silent reassurance. "The board will really lose confidence in me when they find out I'm the one that woman used to gain the access she needed to go after our clients and try to steal our technology. We're talking about a multibillion-dollar company at risk. If it's proven that I made some kind of error in the filing or was careless with my security, they won't care that my last name happens to be on the door. My career will be over here," she said, her anxiety clear.

"But you didn't do anything wrong and we're going to prove it," Francine promised, turning her attention to Robert. "Anything else?"

"There…there was a picture of your father," Robert replied, and the hesitation in his voice and the tense set of his shoulders put Farrah on alert.

Frank Blake, a former Army Ranger and co-founder of Blake & Montgomery, was currently serving as the board's chairman and was a "superhero" to his girls. After suffering from a mild heart attack and at his own family's insistence, Frank had stepped down from his role as CEO and only interacted with company operations on a limited basis. Dealing with their father's illness had been hard. Add that to the danger that Francine had experienced last summer, and the possibility of another member of their family being in harm's way was something they weren't ready for.

At Robert's words, Francine's breath caught and Meeks knelt down beside her. Farrah's knees gave way and Robert helped her into a chair. Farrah felt as if her heart had been struck by a bolt of ice, like a character in a children's movie her sister had recently made her watch. "Our father? How…why? He hasn't played an active role in the company for a couple of years now. And he's just getting back on his feet…he barely leaves the house," Farrah explained, fighting to stay calm.

"What was the picture of, and do we know when it was taken?" Francine asked.

"He was having lunch with your mother. The picture looks old…like it was taken sometime *before* the heart attack," Robert admitted.

"This may not have anything to do with our father, but we're going to find out what really happened. You're not taking the fall for this," Francine insisted, placing her hand on Farrah's shoulder.

"I agree," Meeks echoed.

"Damn right," Robert added, kneeling down before Farrah, bringing their intertwined hands to his chest. He stared into Farrah's eyes. "Sweetheart, I promise, we're going to find out who set this whole thing up. We'll prove our T500 system has nothing to do with those false preliminary designs." Robert kissed her hands. "You didn't miss anything and I'm going to prove it."

Now he shows his faith in me. What happened to that

faith when he stood before the board and requested to have another lawyer come in and replace me on this case?

Francine reached for her sister's hand, which Farrah readily accepted. The declarations made by Robert and the warmth of her sister's hand gave Farrah the strength she needed to pull herself together. The love circling the four of them was like a welcome fog.

Farrah took a deep breath and pulled her hand free of Robert's before standing. "Let's see it. And I mean everything."

"And no holding back," Francine demanded, glaring at her husband.

Robert and Farrah smiled at the "Don't play with me" look Francine was giving Meeks.

"All right, I've printed everything out. Let's move over to the conference table. We'll have more room," Robert explained, bringing several sets of documents and spreading them on the desk.

Meeks helped Francine out of one chair and into another at the head of the table. Francine started sorting through the files that lay before them. "I'm going to need an energy boost if we're going to dig through all this," she said, gesturing toward what could only be a full night's worth of work. She picked up a folder and looked over at Meeks. "Honey, call Paul and have him order some Chinese—he knows what to get—but have him add a large half cheese, half pepperoni pizza."

"That's not Chinese," Robert said, bewilderment in his voice.

"We don't discriminate when it comes to food. Every continent can be spoken for, right, babies?" Francine said, speaking to her stomach. "And tell him to bring down my cookie dough ice cream that's in the freezer in my office when he's done," she said without looking up from the papers she held.

"Seriously?" Farrah asked, frowning at her sister.

"What?" Francine replied as she rubbed her stomach. "We're hungry."

"Dude, where does it all go?" Robert asked Meeks, who laughed as he picked up the phone and punched in Paul's extension.

"Thank you, Robert," Francine said proudly. "Let's get to work. Oh, and honey, tell Paul to bring down some diet Cokes, too."

Everyone laughed.

Chapter 15

Farrah could feel her sister's eyes boring a hole in the red shirt she wore. She looked up from the document she'd been reading. "What?"

Francine was sitting back in her chair, slowly fanning herself with a manila file folder. "You ready to tell me what's really going on between you and Robert?"

"What are you talking about? And why are you doing that?" she asked through narrowed eyes. "It's not even hot in here. Was it all that food you just wolfed down?"

"Being pregnant with twins tends to make you hot from time to time," Francine responded, placing the folder on top of a pile of schematics. "Now stop changing the subject and answer my question before the guys get back from taking out the trash. I caught that sweetheart comment and Robert's uncanny ability to talk you off the ledge like only your sisters can."

Farrah sighed and rubbed her temples.

Busted. Might as well come clean...a little, anyway. "We had a tiny affair," she confessed, using her thumb and index finger to illustrate her point. "But now it's over." Farrah braced herself for her sister's response.

Francine's gaze darted to Farrah's neck which was turning red—a rare occurrence. She checked the office door before locking a steely gaze on Farrah. "Is it? Over, I mean."

That's it? Where's the lecture? "Of course," Farrah offered. "We both wanted a taste, we took it, and now we've moved on."

Francine continued to stare at her sister, but held her tongue. Farrah picked up another file and blindly flipped through the pages of financial records. "I mean, we all know how Robert is when it comes to women. He's never serious. Although..." She flashed back to that place and time in Sugar Land, Texas. "Momma Penny seems to think otherwise. I guess she'd know. And I must admit, he doesn't party as much as he used to."

Francine smiled. "You met *his mother*! Meeks says he never introduces his women to her. Ever!"

Farrah couldn't help but smile. "I know."

"Look at that smile." Francine shimmied a playful little happy dance. "That can only mean one thing. And frankly, it's about time."

Farrah kept her focus on the paper she held, knowing that her smile had only grown wider. She wondered if her sister could hear how fast her heart was beating all the way across the table.

"What's about time?" Meeks asked as he walked into the office with Robert on his heels. He kissed the top of his wife's head before taking the seat next to her.

"Nothing," Farrah quickly interjected, sitting up in her chair. "Now that the twins have been fortified and the trash has been removed from the building, can we please get back to work?"

Robert came around the table and settled into the space next to Farrah.

"All right, we've been through all these files, so what do we know so far?" Meeks asked.

"We know that Alexia made a fortune either black-mailing folks or trying to sell their secrets," Farrah said, tapping her pen on the table.

"That she did," Robert agreed.

"We need to figure out who all these other people are in her records and what their current status is," Francine added.

"Besides that," Meeks said, stroking his hand across the silky material over his wife's stomach, "we know her right-hand man is Butch Johnson from New Orleans. She's paid him a lot of money for who knows what."

"He may be able to fill in some of the blanks regarding all these other people, too," Robert said as he scanned the final columns of a financial spreadsheet.

"Thankfully, Butch Johnson was easy to find, and our team has him on lock until you make it down there," Meeks said.

"I'll work on getting access to Alexia," Francine said, looking at her sister. "I think you're right. We have to use Blige as leverage."

"Good. What about Trey? I think I should run by his place and bring him up to speed on these new developments," she offered, rising from her chair.

"Hell, no!" Robert snapped, causing Meeks and Francine to flinch. Farrah could almost see the anger radiating from Robert's body.

"Excuse me?" Farrah said, whipping her head in his direction.

"I just don't think that's necessary...not just yet, anyway," Robert replied, less forcefully this time.

"Yet you found it necessary to bring him on in the first place, didn't you?"

Robert held up his hands in mock surrender. "We've discussed this already. I found it necessary to bring in someone *like* him. You chose that muscled-up, dark-eyed Perry Mason wannabe. I was thinking of someone more along the lines of Ben Matlock."

"Really?" Farrah said, her head at an angle. "You're actually comparing Trey to television characters? He's an exceptional attorney who's argued before both the State and Federal Supreme Courts and won...twice. You wanted someone more experienced handling our case. Well, Trey fits the bill perfectly in spite of how young, fine and handsome he may be."

Robert looked fiercely down at Farrah, but held his tongue.

Meeks leaned over to Francine and whispered loud enough for the others to hear, "I think we need some popcorn for this."

"I ate it all," Francine mumbled, eliciting a hearty chuckle from Meeks.

Farrah straightened her head and narrowed her eyes, sending a steely glare in Robert's direction and asking, "When do you suggest we—"

"When we know more," Robert interjected, holding Farrah's gaze.

Meeks checked his watch. "It's almost nine. You ready to head upstairs?" he asked Francine.

"Yes, and if you're lucky, these two will sleep long enough for me to put you to bed properly," she said, giving her husband a wicked smile. Meeks kissed her passionately before leading her out of the office.

Even angry, Farrah's heart ached for Robert. She'd never been jealous of either of her sisters, but in that moment, she wished she could take Robert upstairs and put *him* to sleep properly. "Look, regardless of how Trey got here, and—"

"And it was the best move for all concerned. Imagine what would have happened if you'd still been the attorney of record when all this bogus evidence came out."

Farrah bit her bottom lip and after a few moments gave Robert a reluctant nod. Robert stood and gave her a lengthy once-over. "Look, when we have something firm, we'll share it. For now, I think I'll head down to the gym. Care to join me?" he asked.

"No, thanks," she said, stacking the files. "I think I'll take some of this stuff upstairs with me for a little late-night reading."

"We've been over all of those a thousand times. Security's in place in New Orleans and we can't do anything until tomorrow. We've got everything covered, so why don't you take a break? I'll blow off the gym and if you like, we can go check out this new spot not far from my place." Robert gifted her with a sexy smile. "We could have a couple of drinks, talk, or even dance."

Farrah returned his smile and leaned back in her chair. "You know, a night out…a change in scenery could do me some good."

"See, that wasn't so hard to admit," he replied, offering a wink and a smile.

"Give me forty-five minutes to go upstairs and change."

"No problem. That'll give me time to run home, change and meet you downstairs."

Farrah collected her things and headed for the door. "It's only a drink between friends," she whispered to herself, trying to keep her excitement and traitorous body under control.

She felt as if a live wire had been lit inside her heart at the mere thought of what the evening could bring.

Chapter 16

Robert sat back in his chair as the private jet took off down the Hobby Airport runway. He glanced at Farrah, who was stretched out in her reclined seat with her eyes closed and her body covered by a Burberry blanket. Robert couldn't help but smile as he thought back on last night's activities that caused Farrah's current state and need for a nap.

"You just had to wear that outfit, didn't you?" Robert asked, glaring down at Farrah as he pulled out her chair, allowing his gaze to sweep the room. He could see the envy in the eyes of every man in the place.

Farrah removed her jacket and took her seat. "This is an Alexander McQueen original," she said, gesturing to the outfit. "What's wrong with it?"

"Oh, I don't know, maybe the fact that it's a one-piece halter pant-suit thing that fits you like a second skin, showing off that fabulous body of yours." Robert took

the seat directly next to hers. "Not to mention there's no back, and the front is open down damn near to your navel. A very cute navel, I might add. I just might spend most of the night fighting off the guys."

Farrah laughed. "Good thing I can take care of myself. Don't worry." She gave his arm a quick pat. "I got your back, just like you've always had mine."

A moment of silence ensued before he said, "You look breathtakingly beautiful tonight." Robert ran the back of his hand slowly down the side of her face. "I love it when you wear your hair down."

"I know," she said barely above a whisper before gifting him with a slow sexy smile.

Robert's eyes dropped to her mouth and like a magnet, he felt himself being pulled forward. His lips grazed the corner of her mouth. Their eyes met and for the first time, Robert saw emotions she failed to hide and was suddenly given an inkling of encouragement. In that moment, it was as if they were the only two people in the room. Before Robert could act on his raging need, a young blonde approached their table.

"Welcome to Believe." The petite ivory-skinned woman began removing the contents of a silver tray and placing them on the table next to several small containers that held limes, lemons, olives and salt. She placed a bucket of ice, two small bottles of orange and cranberry juices, glasses and two pint-size alcohol bottles in the center of the table—tequila and vodka. "Enjoy."

"What's all this?" Farrah asked with one raised eyebrow.

"Believe is a private club. Members only, and this bottle service setup is standard."

Her gaze swept over the items that lay before them. "But what if I want something else?"

Robert picked up her hand and kissed the inside of her palm. "Sweetheart, you can have anything you like."

"Well, in that case." Farrah poured them both a shot of tequila and raised her glass. "Bottoms up."

After another round of drinks and listening to Farrah break down the club's contemporary style and unique seating throughout the place, Robert finally had Farrah in his arms when the DJ played a slow song. He didn't even try to fight his body's response to her closeness. Robert wanted her to know what she did to him. He would give anything to take her home and bury himself deep inside her; however, he couldn't quite do that. Not yet, anyway. Instead, he spent the next few painful hours making sure Farrah relaxed, had fun, and knew she had his undivided attention.

"We have an early flight," Robert reminded Farrah. "In about four hours, so we should call it a night. Besides, I think you've had more than enough."

"Do you now?" Farrah said, the corners of her mouth rising slightly.

"Damn, you're beautiful," he said.

"You're pretty beautiful yourself," she answered, her smile widening.

Robert took Farrah by the hand and led her out of the club and to his waiting car. Determined to prove that she could trust him with her heart, Robert saw Farrah to her door and gave her a tame kiss on the lips. He bid her good-night and started backing away from her.

"You want to come in for a nightcap...or something?" Farrah asked, leaning against her doorjamb.

Robert had to flex every muscle he had in order to stop himself from charging forward. "It's late, and I don't think you really want that."

Farrah straightened her stance and placed her right

hand on her hip. "You don't think I know my own mind?" *she challenged.*

Robert closed the space between them and took her into his arms. He stared into her eyes for several moments before devouring her mouth with a kiss that left no doubt about how much he wanted her. He released her mouth so they could both take a breath. They were breathing hard as he leaned his forehead against hers. "I have no doubt that you know your own mind. What I need is for you to know your heart. The way I know mine because the next time I take you to bed, I won't be leaving it...ever!" Robert kissed Farrah on the cheek, turned and walked away, a Herculean effort whose ache even a cold shower couldn't assuage.

The landing gear hitting the runway at New Orleans's Louis Armstrong Airport brought Robert back to the present. Robert reached over and shook Farrah awake. "We're here, sleepyhead," Robert said, offering her a cup of coffee with her favorite vanilla creamer and holding out two pain relievers.

Farrah sighed and released a soft moan before slowly opening her eyes. She gave him a relieved smile as she accepted his offerings. "Bless you." Farrah tossed back the pills and took a few sips of coffee to wash them down.

"How's your head?" Robert asked, trying not to smile but failing miserably.

"Don't gloat. It's not a good look."

Farrah finished her coffee before getting to her feet. "Give me ten minutes to freshen up and we can go."

"Take all the time you need. Butch Johnson isn't going anywhere," he called after Farrah as he watched her walk toward the bedrooms in the rear of the plane. "Down, boy," Robert whispered to himself.

* * *

Thirty minutes later, Robert, Farrah and two members of their team exited two black SUVs in front of a strip club off Bourbon Street. The name of the club was Dream's; only the sign outside was missing the letters *e* and *m*.

"This is the place?" Farrah asked, directing her question to no one in particular.

"Yes, ma'am, this is it," said one of the agents from the security detail they'd brought to ensure Butch Johnson didn't take off. "He's inside…in the back office."

"Thanks," she said.

"You stay put," Robert added.

"Seriously?" Farrah murmured as they entered the empty space, taking notice of the dilapidated furnishings. They walked past a small stage and bar before entering a back room, where they found a man with a medium build, dark complexion and short brown hair sitting at a small wood table. The windowless room was dimly lit and smelled of stale cigarettes and alcohol. A small desk was situated in one corner of the room with a shabby, half-closed sleeper sofa in the other.

The man sat with his hands clasped in front of him, bouncing his right leg under the table. Butch Johnson looked uncomfortable surrounded by five people all wearing the standard Blake & Montgomery uniform with guns on their hips. Robert stood with his feet apart and arms folded, a stance that most found intimidating but Farrah thought was a sexy turn-on.

Farrah took the seat across from Butch. "Guys, can you give us the room, please?" she asked without taking her eyes off the man who she believed held the key to unlocking their mystery. Farrah waited until the room was cleared before she made the introductions. "Mr. Johnson, my name is Farrah Blake, and this menacing-looking gentleman behind me is Robert Gold."

"Will someone tell me what the hell is going on here?" he demanded. "What do you people want from me?"

"Mr. Johnson…may I call you Butch?" Farrah asked.

"Yeah," he replied.

"Good. And I'm Farrah." Farrah crossed her legs and sat back in her chair. "Butch, are you trying to tell me that you have no idea why we're here?"

"Umm…no, not really," he said, his eyes darting from Farrah to Robert.

Robert tilted his head and narrowed his eyes, but remained silent.

"I guess you could be looking for information about Al…I mean, Alexia Gray." Butch leaned forward and shrugged his shoulders—bravado on full display.

"And you're right. You see, Alexia was hired to steal a lot of information from our company and plant false evidence. I want to know who hired her and why."

"I don't know anything—"

Farrah held up her hand to stop his denial. "Before you say anything else, let me tell you what we already know." Farrah uncrossed her legs and sat forward with her arms resting on the table. "Alexia was asked to plant a specific set of forged documents in our system. What I need to know is who hired her and why?"

"Look, I swear—"

"Don't!" Farrah waggled a finger in his direction. "We tracked the money. It flowed through several shell companies and dummy accounts. One of those companies was this lovely establishment of yours. In fact, this place received over two million dollars. You really should've considered putting some of that money in the décor. That would've made it more believable."

Robert smirked.

"I'm telling you, I don't know anything about Alexia's business," he said, running a shaking hand through his hair.

"Let me tell you what I think," Farrah said, shifting her gaze from the table to his dark brown eyes. "You either know who paid for her services or you can get us close to them. I also think you can give us the forger. Your colorful past would suggest you'd know such a person. Now, you can either tell me," she said, pointing to herself. "Or I can leave and you can talk to Robert. And trust me when I say he won't ask nearly as nicely as I have."

Butch's mouth remained still. Farrah sighed and stood. "Oh, well, I tried. Robert, maybe you can talk some sense into him." Farrah turned to leave as Robert took a step forward. "Don't make a mess."

"Wait!" Butch released a deep sigh, dropped his shoulders and sat back in his chair. "Ruby Lee."

"Ruby Lee?" Robert asked, frowning down at Butch.

"Ruby Lee...she set everything up."

"How did she find you?" Farrah asked. "Somehow you're listed in the yellow pages under criminals for hire?"

Robert smirked as he gave his head a slow shake.

"No, like you said, I have a colorful history. People know who to come to when they want to get things done. You all found your way down here, didn't ya?" Butch asked, shrugging.

Farrah returned to her chair. "How can we find this Ruby Lee?"

"I have a cell phone number," he offered, pulling out his phone where he began scrolling through his contacts. "But I don't know if it's still good. It was probably a burner phone."

"How were the payments made?" Robert inquired.

"Cash, except for the initial payment. *That* was done by a wire transfer."

Robert and Farrah shared a knowing glance, but it was Robert who asked, "Do you still have the banking information from where it was sent?"

Butch sighed again. "Yeah."

Farrah glanced at Robert and grinned. Once they had that number, they could trace it back to where the money came from, and hopefully to the person making the transfer. Another piece of the puzzle would fall into place, and they'd be that much closer to making sure the damage done by Alexia's deception had been kept to a minimum.

Chapter 17

They sat in the back of the SUV in silence as they made their way back to the airport. All Farrah could think about was tracking down whoever it was threatening her company. But that was interrupted when she suddenly felt Robert's eyes burning a hole in the side of her face. Farrah sent Robert a sideways glance. "What?"

"You…that's what," he shot back. "I can feel you thinking over here. Spit it out. What's going on?"

Farrah rubbed her hands together. "That name, Ruby Lee. It seems familiar."

"Maybe you ran across it in some of Alexia's documents," he suggested as he pulled his phone from his pocket.

"What are you doing?"

"Running the name through a quick scan of all the documents," he explained, tapping a few of the keys. "I had them filtered, tagged, and saved as a searchable file that I can access from my phone."

"You can do that?" she asked, her eyes widening in shock.

Robert's forehead creased and he just stared at her.

Farrah raised her hands. "Excuse me."

"Nope, there's no mention of a Ruby Lee in anything we got off the drive. There wasn't a mention of Butch, either. I'll get the team on it." Robert put in his earpiece, then dialed.

"I know that name," she murmured to herself. Farrah's phone vibrated with a text from Francine. "Yes!"

"What's up?" Robert asked as he put his phone away.

"Francine got us in to see Alexia tomorrow afternoon."

"That should be interesting," he said. Robert reached over and took Farrah's hand in his and ran his thumb slowly across her palm.

Farrah laid her head back against the seat and offered him a slight smile, trying to control her escalating heartbeat which caused her breasts to rise and fall faster than normal—a reaction to his touch. To ensure that he couldn't be heard, Robert leaned over and whispered, "Have dinner with me tonight…at my place."

Fighting the desire to lean in and answer Robert with a kiss, Farrah bit her lip and slowly nodded. Robert brought her hand to his mouth and kissed it before sitting back in the seat and watched as she closed her eyes, keeping his hand in hers.

Two hours later, Robert opened the door and leaned against his doorjamb. His gaze swept over Farrah's body, every masculine cell coming to attention. She wore blue jeans and a matching jean jacket with a red V-neck Texans T-shirt underneath and a pair of wedge-heel tennis shoes. "Even when you dress down, you're sexy beautiful."

"Thank you," she said, giving him a once-over.

"You're not too shabby yourself. Well, except for your choice in shirts." Robert was wearing low-riding jeans and a Dallas Cowboys T-shirt, a move he knew she'd find irritating since the Cowboys were a rival team.

Robert laughed. "Please come in." He waved his hand in front of him and stepped aside. Robert closed the door and followed Farrah into the open-concept living and kitchen space. The dark hardwood floors, leather and wood furnishings screamed "alpha male cave."

"I see not much has changed." Farrah took a seat on an extra-large sectional sofa situated near the large bay window and in front of his entertainment wall. She looked up and focused on one thing in particular. "Nothing's changed, except for that antique double ceiling fan that I could've sworn was in your office this afternoon."

"It still is. I bought another one for my house."

Farrah threw her head back and laughed.

"What's so funny? I love that fan," he said, favoring her with a grin.

"I know, that's what's so funny," she countered. "Paul seems to think we have a lot in common, and spending money on things like that is one of them."

"Does he now?" Farrah noticed the spark in his eyes that he didn't even try to hide. "You'd do the same thing if you found something you loved that much. You wouldn't let anything stop you from claiming it as your own…"

For a moment they just looked at each other. Then he broke that gaze, picked up two of the four bottles that had been chilling in the silver ice bucket on the coffee table. "Beer?"

"Please."

Robert twisted off the tops and handed one to Farrah. He raised his bottle and said, "To a very nice evening."

Farrah smiled, raised her bottle and gave a slow single

nod before taking a drink. "So, unless you've added a new ventilation system, too, I don't smell anything cooking and I'm hungry."

Robert leaned forward, resting his forearms against one of the tall leather wingback chairs. "I invited you to have dinner *at* my place. I didn't say I would be cooking it."

"All right, so what do you have in mind?" she asked, taking another sip of her beer.

"I ordered barbecue ribs from your favorite spot," he explained proudly.

Farrah sat up straight, her eyes widened and her eyebrows stood at attention. "Since when did they start delivering to residences?"

"They don't. Roger's bringing it to us."

"Roger, from Green's team? Why?" she asked, tilting her head.

"He was getting something for himself and his family. It's his night to cook," Robert explained, laughing. "And he offered to bring me something, too. I took him up on his offer and bought their dinner along with ours."

"That was nice of him…and you." Farrah gifted Robert with a sexy smile.

Robert's heart skipped several beats. *This woman!* He stood and made his way around the chair; it was as though Farrah's smile and eyes were beckoning him forward. Before he could take another step in her direction, there was a knock on the door.

"Right on time," Farrah teased, causing Robert to give her the evil eye as he shifted direction and went for the door.

Farrah stood. "I'll get some plates. I assume we're eating here in front of this massive entertainment center of yours so we can watch the Texans beat the pants off the Cowboys while we eat."

"You assume correctly on one point," he said over his shoulder. "But it's the Cowboys who are going to serve the Texans their asses on a plate."

Farrah returned with plates and utensils just as Robert started pulling stiff white boxes out of the bags. "So what's all this?" she asked, surveying all the containers.

"We have ribs, of course, potato salad, baked beans and peach cobbler for dessert."

"It all smells so good," she said, inhaling the wonderful aromas. "You really did think of everything."

Robert gazed into Farrah's eyes. "I sincerely hope so." He grabbed the remote and flipped on the TV. "May the best team win."

"We will," she said, flashing him a winning smile. "Because it's going to be the Texans all day long."

Robert and Farrah ate as they watched the game, both coaching their teams from their respective seats and teasing each other on the side. The night was all about fun, football, trading sports insults, and stuffing themselves on great food. In between, they held hands, shared sweet caresses and a few benign kisses. In spite of the sexual tension that floated along the surface of the evening, Robert managed to keep things light. At the end of the night, he held Farrah's hand as they walked to her car.

"Tonight was fun. Too bad my team came up short, but we'll get them next time," she challenged.

"I'm *sure* you will," he said sarcastically.

"Gloating…still not a good look."

Robert held up his right hand as though swearing. "Never."

"If I didn't know any better, I'd say we just had our first date."

"Would that be so bad?" Robert asked, leaning against her car before pulling Farrah down with him and into his arms.

"Not at all," she said, smiling up at him. "After all, we did get married."

"Well, giving you a good date is the least I can do," he said, capturing her lips in the most passionate kiss they'd shared all night.

"Wow," Farrah murmured, blinking rapidly after taking a breath.

Robert helped her into the car. "Drive safe." He closed her door and stood with his hands in his pockets, watching her drive away. Once she was out of sight, Robert ran back into the house and straight to his bathroom, where he took a long, cold shower.

Farrah walked ahead of her sister into one of the small prisoner-interrogation rooms offered by the Harris County Jail system. She wore a navy blue Chanel suit with her hair pulled back in a tight bun, while Francine had on a tan pleated maternity dress. The small, whitewalled room had a two-way mirror, a metal table with four matching chairs and another door in the center of the back wall.

Francine took a seat and crossed her legs at her ankles before clasping her hands over her stomach. She released a small sigh, tucked her hair behind both ears and smiled up at her sister. "All right, Farrah, we've got thirty minutes and we're here to be reasonable," Francine beseeched her sister.

"Reasonable? You should have stayed in your car if you wanted to be reasonable," she shot back. "We're here to get some answers."

Before Francine had an opportunity to reply to Farrah's statement, the second door in the room opened and two stocky guards walked in, escorting a handcuffed Alexia Gray. She wore the required orange jumpsuit and her long dark hair was plaited in a single braid that hung down her back. Even in chains and enhanced by no makeup, the dark-eyed, olive-skinned woman looked beautiful. Alexia stopped the moment she saw the sisters. She turned her back on both women and demanded, "Take me back. I've changed my mind. I don't want to talk to them."

"Not even to hear a message from Blige?" Farrah offered, shifting her weight to her left foot, placing her right hand on her hip.

Alexia quickly turned back around. *"Blige,"* she whispered. "You have a message from Blige?" Her gaze narrowed to slits. "How did you even know about her, let alone find her?"

Farrah gestured to the chair across from Francine. "Come in and I'll fill you in. Otherwise, you can return to your cell and wait for your trial to find out everything we know." Farrah looked at her sister. "What, that's like a year away at least, right?"

"At least," Francine said, keeping her focus on Alexia.

"I'm not talking to both of you," Alexia said, breaking eye contact with Francine and returning her attention to Farrah.

"That's not your call," Farrah shot back.

Alexia smirked as though she knew something they didn't. "Is that so…"

Francine stood and held up her right hand to stop the tirade she knew her sister was gearing up to rain down on Alexia. "I understand. I imagine it's hard to face even one person whose life you tried to destroy, let alone two," she said to Alexia, who refused to meet her gaze.

"We don't have a lot of time and I don't need to be here for this. I'm sure you have everything under control." Francine picked up her purse and turned to her sister. "Beside, we're hungry, so I'll meet you back at my place later."

Farrah nodded. "Good thing you drove. That way, you don't have to wait to get those tacos you and those babies love so much."

"Don't get too crazy," Francine warned as she walked out of the room.

"I make no promises," Farrah said, smiling at the familiar advice.

Chapter 18

Alexia frowned at Farrah, glaring. "What do you want? If it was your plan to humiliate me—fine. Just deliver your message from Blige and leave," she commanded.

"I don't give a damn about your humiliation. That's just an added bonus," Farrah countered, taking the seat vacated by her sister. "No, I actually care about that poor girl you've pulled into your mess."

Alexia followed her lead, taking the chair across from her. "Blige has nothing to do with my business," she said, placing her handcuffed hands on the table.

"That's not how the district attorney sees it. In fact, he's ready to kill two birds with one stone. After all, that flash drive you left with her for safekeeping has enough evidence on it to put you both away for a very long time."

"Me, not Blige," she said, leaning back in the chair.

Farrah had to knock that relaxed look off Alexia's face if she wanted to get the information she needed.

"She had the evidence. Even after we round up all of your clients and partners in crime, that still might not be enough for him. Blige could have a lot of explaining to do," Farrah said, finally seeing a flash of anxiety on the other woman's face.

"What do you want?" Alexia asked, sitting up in her chair.

Farrah slammed her fist against the table. "You know *damn* well what I want," she said through her teeth. "I want to know who hired you to destroy our business and why. I want the forger. And I especially want to know how you got past all my security."

Alexia leaned forward, a sly smile on her heart-shaped face. "You're a smart girl. I thought you would've figured all that out by now."

Farrah stood, placed both palms flat on the table and stared down at Alexia. "I'm done playing games with you. You have five minutes to tell me everything I want to know, and I mean *everything*, or so help me, I'm going to make sure they arrest Blige as an accessory after the fact and a host of other things I'm sure I can come up with," she said. "Then I'll make sure they put her in a place where she can spend some quality time with women that will make sure she's ready for prison when the time comes."

Even speaking such a threat caused Farrah's anxiety to whip around in her belly like a hurricane. While it killed her to go this route, it was the only way to move Alexia. There was too much at stake for her not to use all the weapons at her disposal. Farrah could only hope that Alexia bought it because she didn't think she could deliver anything more.

All the color drained from Alexia's face and her shoulders drooped in defeat. "I'll give you what you want. Just leave Blige out of this."

Farrah returned to the seat. "On my word of honor, I'll make sure no one ever finds out anything about Blige and that she spends the next few years safe, happy and enjoying the college experience."

Alexia settled back in her chair. "How do I know I can trust you?"

Farrah raised her chin slightly. "I'm not the criminal in this scenario, remember?" she reminded through tight lips. "We found the forged documents. Who hired you to plant them? Are there any other attacks that I should know about? And is there someone out there picking up where you left off?" Farrah crossed her arms, a move she used to hide her trembling hands. She didn't want Alexia to see how much that thought scared her. But Alexia's silence worried her even more. "Start talking…now."

Alexia looked down at her cuffed hands. "People who hire me don't need backups. I'm usually pretty exceptional at what I do. However, I can't speak for what they're doing now that I'm…unavailable," Alexia explained, lifting her gaze to meet Farrah's, her lips spreading into a smile.

Farrah stared at Alexia, fighting the urge to ask the guards to give her five minutes alone with her. "Who… hired you?"

"I was hired by a middle man—or should I say, a middle woman. Her name is—"

"Ruby Lee," Farrah offered, shifting a little in her chair.

"Yes but I don't think that's her real name. Check my files—"

"We did that already. I need more," Farrah demanded.

"Look for a zip file on Lee Rugby," she insisted. "It's listed under my past clients. Everything you need to find her is there—bank account information, photos and multiple phone numbers." Alexia glared at Farrah. "But be warned, she's just the broker and she has a special kind of loyalty to her client. I don't think she has anyone you can use against her like you're using Blige against me," she said sarcastically.

"We'll see about that." Farrah stood to leave. "Not that you deserve this, but a deal's a deal. Blige sends her love and she's grateful for everything you've done for her. She says you're like a sister to her. She's really worried about you. I tried to assure her you were fine, but she's just a kid, so…"

Alexia turned her head away. After a few moments, she used her forearm to wipe away wayward tears. In spite of all the damage Alexia had caused, Farrah couldn't help but feel sorry for her. The woman was losing someone she clearly cared about. "Look, it's obvious you care about Blige."

Alexia leaned back in her chair and stared at Farrah through narrowed eyes. "You don't know a damn thing about me…about us."

"There she is." Farrah stood with her right hand on her hip. "That nasty woman with an evil soul that I hate with—"

"Right back at you," she spat back. "You just be sure to keep your end of the deal."

"Oh, I will. And if there's any love left for that sweet girl in that horrible heart of yours, you would call her. Tell her to move on with her life and forget all about you," she said, pointing at her. "I'm going to do everything in my power to keep her out of this mess and so should you," Farrah said before walking out the door.

Francine stared at the six different shades of beige and gray paints on the wall earmarked as the accent wall and rubbed her belly. "All right, guys, what do you think?

Daddy says they're all basically the same colors but he doesn't know what he's talking about."

Farrah walked into the enormous baby suite and gasped. "Are you crazy? Of course you are, you're talking to yourself," she taunted as she rushed to her sister's side. "Why on earth are you standing on a stepladder holding a paintbrush? Should you even be around those fumes?"

Francine's forehead crumpled. She reluctantly took her sister's hand and let her guide her down the two steps. "First of all, I wasn't talking to myself. I was talking to my babies. Second, I was barely off the ground and the paint's not toxic. There isn't even a smell," Francine said, settling into one of the four matching wingback rocking chairs.

Farrah sat in the chair next to her sister, kicked off her shoes and took a deep breath. "You're right, there isn't a smell. Now why do you have four of the exact same style rocking chair?"

Francine laughed. "You sound like Meeks. I liked both the gray and the cream, but I wasn't sure which one I wanted to go with, so I decided what the hell, and got them both." She leaned back and slowly started to rock. "Enough of all that, so tell me what happened? What did you find out?"

Farrah spent the next twenty minutes rehashing her discussion with Alexia, including the threat she'd had to make against Blige. "I still feel sick about having to say those things about Blige." Farrah rubbed her temples with both hands.

"That kid really got to you, didn't she?" Francine asked, her eyebrows standing at attention.

"I guess so. I did a little research on her and even though she was an only child, she wasn't spoiled. She seemed to have had a normal, happy life until she lost her parents in that car crash."

"How did she get mixed up with Alexia in the first place?"

Farrah shrugged. "All I know is that Alexia did some type of work for her parents. So I guess she felt some kind of concern about the fact that she was orphaned and took her in. Set up a lucrative trust fund for her and sent her to school."

Francine's gaze fell to the massive wedding ring resting on her left finger before scanning the different-sized family photos that covered nearly every wall and ultimately landing on the two Mommy's & Daddy's Angel shirts she'd recently purchased. All signs of parents who wanted to provide a happy beginning for the children they were bringing into the world. "I agree. We should keep an eye on her. Make sure she stays out of trouble and doesn't let what Alexia did become her path in life." Francine released a deep sigh. "Now, what are we doing to find Lee Rugby?"

"Robert's going back over the files now."

"Robert..." Francine sang.

"Yes. Robert...and why are you singing his name and looking at me like that?"

"Oh, I don't know, maybe because your face seems to light up whenever you're around him these days. Has anything changed on that front?"

Farrah exhaled noisily, realizing that her sister wouldn't let it go until she got answered. "We had dinner and watched the game at his place last night, and it was fun."

"That's good."

"I guess," she replied, looking down at her hands.

"What is it?"

"Nothing…it's just…" Farrah closed her eyes briefly. "Nothing's happening. I mean, he kissed me a few times, but then he walked me to my car and sent me home."

"So…"

"I just thought…" She paused as several wicked scenarios whipped through her mind. "Never mind what I thought."

"You thought you'd be rocking the sheets before halftime," Francine said, bursting into laughter. "Didn't he say he wanted more from you than just sex?"

"Yes, but—"

"And didn't you say there's more to him than you thought?" She held up her hand. "Don't say a word because we both know the answer."

Farrah huffed.

"So why are you trying to keep him in that shallow box that he clearly doesn't belong in? Let the man show you he can offer you more than—"

"A series of amazing orgasms," she replied, placing a dramatic hand over her heart.

"I'm serious," Francine said.

"So am I."

"I'm going to give you the same advice you gave me about Meeks a while ago," Francine said, pulling down the light throw blanket from the back of her chair and adjusting it over her stomach. "It's pretty obvious that you two have some seriously intense feelings for each other. In fact, I think you're in love with him and that scares the hell out of you."

Farrah gave a noncommittal shrug.

"I know you're still angry about him forcing the board to bring in another attorney to handle the case, but you do see he was only trying to protect you…and your career, right?" Francine's eyebrows furrowed. "And it's a good thing he did, too, considering everything we've found."

"If we can't prove that I wasn't negligent in my initial work and security, my career will be damaged anyway," she said, resting her head back against the chair.

"Don't worry, sis. Everything's going to be fine. Of course, that will mean Robert was right about his instinct to protect you."

"I know," she said in a voice barely above a whisper.

Francine chuckled as she said, "I hate it when Meeks is right, too." She chortled. "Sweetie, I just want you to be happy. I think you should follow your own advice and let go of your fears. Talk to Robert. You might be surprised by the results. Now, come help me out of my chair so I can go make us a snack. I'm hungry."

"You're always hungry," Farrah shot back.

"It's not me…it's them."

"Hmm." Farrah smiled as she watched Francine walk out of the nursery, talking to her babies as she was left with thoughts of the last time she followed her sister's advice and let go.

Vegas…

Chapter 19

"You want some peach tea?" Farrah heard her sister ask, breaking her connection to the past.

"Umm…what?"

Francine's forehead creased with worry. "What in the world were you just thinking about? You're all red…and blushing."

"Nothing, it's just hot in—"

"No, it's not," Francine shot back, her frown deepening.

"I have to go," she said, checking the wall clock, thankful that their triplet connection was off today; otherwise, Francine would have a pretty good idea as to why she was blushing. "I have to get back to the office. I have a meeting with Fletcher Scott."

Francine's head whipped to Farrah. "Fletcher? Why, what's up?"

"I'm having him check into something for Felicia. No big deal."

"We sure keep Fletcher busy with all our personal stuff, don't we? What's going on?" Francine asked, taking her seat again.

"Do you remember Felicia's old medical school roommate, Valarie Washington?"

Francine nodded. "The girl who Felicia called Mega-Brain because she never really studied. She just really seemed to know the answers to everything."

"That's the one," Farrah confirmed. "Well, she died and left our baby sister her estate…her multimillion-dollar estate," she said, placing her hand on her hip.

"She died?" Francine whispered. "I'm sorry to hear that. How?"

"Cancer…unfortunately."

"I remember her being really cool. Wait, did you say her estate?" Francine asked, rubbing her sides with the palms of her hands. "If I remember correctly, she was a foster kid going to school on the state's dime and scholarships. I think she became a pediatrician. Wow, she must've done really well for herself."

"She did, but the money came from her husband. She married well and divorced even better."

"So what are you having Fletcher looking into?"

"The firm that's handling the estate," Farrah replied, gathering her things to leave. "We just need to make sure everything's on the up-and-up before Felicia travels across the world for the appointment."

"Why can't you just handle it for her?"

"One of the stipulations in the will is that she show up in person to collect her inheritance."

"I see."

Farrah offered her sister her hand. "Need help getting up before I go? I'd hate to think of you stuck in that chair until Meeks or Peggy gets back," she teased.

"I'm fine, thank you very much," Francine said in a sour tone. "I can get myself up. It'll just take a minute… or two…" she grimaced, adding, "…or three. You must've really been lost in your thoughts not to hear Peggy return several minutes ago. She's putting away the groceries and finishing up my snack." Francine put her feet up on the chair's matching ottoman. "I swear she's just as bad at hovering as Meeks."

"Why did he insist on hiring you a babysitter anyway? Everyone's either a phone call or elevator ride away."

"The closer I get to my due date, the more worried he becomes," she replied. "Since he can't be with me twenty-four-seven, and with the new celebrity protection case in full swing, he can't put an agent on me, Peggy is the next best thing. Besides, marriage is as much about compromise as it is about making each other happy," Francine stated, rocking. "It makes him happy, knowing Peggy is here helping me out when he's not. I compromised by allowing him to hire her for a few hours a day." Francine picked up the teddy bear that sat on the side table and stroked the soft material. "Anyway, she's sweet and very helpful."

"I guess…"

"Don't forget about what we discussed earlier," Francine reminded as she stopped rocking.

Farrah leaned down and kissed her sister on the cheek. "How could I? Talk to you later."

Robert walked past several midlevel cubicles, heading to his office. As he approached the frosted glass conference room, a familiar voice caught his attention. He turned and entered the conference room. "Fletcher, what are you—"

Fletcher held up his cell phone and Robert stopped

his progression, crossed his arms and waited as the other man completed the call. After a few moments, Fletcher placed his phone in his jacket pocket. "Hey, man, what's up?"

"Just trying to keep the unnecessary from becoming necessary," Robert replied, extending his hand to shake Fletcher's.

Fletcher placed his portfolio on the conference room table. "Well, there's no one better at keeping situations calm and from escalating to World War V than you and your team around here," he replied, accepting Robert's hand.

"Last time I checked, America's only fought in three wars," Robert corrected.

"I meant Francine and Farrah," he said, scratching his bald head. "You know what they're like."

Robert broke into hearty laughter. "So, what are you doing here?"

Fletcher scratched his neck. "Farrah called and asked me to stop by."

"Why?"

"I'm not sure," Fletcher said. "She just said there was something she wanted to talk to me about." He leaned in to whisper. "You don't think she figured it out, do you?"

"No, I'm sure she hasn't," Robert reassured, but inwardly cringed at the thought.

"Because those papers won't stand up to her microscopic inspection," Fletcher warned.

Robert stood and jammed his hands in his pockets. "Like I already told you, Farrah didn't even look at them when I handed it to her. We've been so busy dealing with things around here that I doubt she's even thought about them again."

Fletcher stood up straight and folded his arms across

his chest. "That's all well and good, but I think you need to come clean and tell Farrah the truth."

"Tell me the truth about what exactly?" Farrah asked, standing in the door of the conference room.

Chapter 20

Robert felt as if his stomach was trying to make a break for the Texas hills through his mouth. He glanced briefly at Fletcher before turning his attention to Farrah. "That my...that my net worth is substantially more than you initially thought," he confessed, trying to filter through the most believable scenario possible. "Fletcher thinks that should be made clear to you since we didn't have a pre-nup and you're entitled to some of it." He swept a gaze across her expressionless face. "I have absolutely no problem giving you anything you want."

Farrah gave a dismissive shake of her head as she entered the room and placed her electronic tablet and phone on the conference table. "Oh, well, thanks for thinking of me, Fletcher, but we all know money isn't an issue for me."

Fletcher gave Robert a sideways glance before he said, "I get that, but I wouldn't feel right if I didn't advise you of your rights as his wife."

"We all know we weren't married long enough for either of us to have any rights over the other," Farrah said.

"That's not exactly true," Fletcher said, grinning at Robert, who was holding his breath. "By my account, he could write you a check right now with a whole lot of zeroes…at least seven."

"That won't be necessary," Farrah replied.

"If you insist," he said, shifting his weight from one leg to the other. "So what can I do for you?"

Farrah glanced at Robert. "Well, I'll leave you two to it," he said, getting up to leave.

"There's no need for you to leave. Please…stay," Farrah said, sitting at the conference table as both men followed suit.

Robert glanced at Fletcher, who gestured to the seat next to Farrah.

Farrah spent the next several minutes going over Felicia's request and everything she knew so far. Inwardly, Robert breathed a sigh of relief with every detail spilling out. Although Fletcher had assured Robert that their secret was safe, he was beginning to wonder if it was.

"So Felicia had no idea that she was named in this person's will?" Fletcher asked, scribbling the last of his notes on a tablet.

"None, and before she travels halfway around the world to take the meeting, we want to make sure everything's straightforward."

"No problem. Should I send my report directly to Felicia?" Fletcher asked.

"Yes, but as her attorney, you should copy me in, as well," she confirmed.

Fletcher nodded and stood. "I'm on it."

Farrah stood and shook Fletcher's hand. "Thank you, and we appreciate your discretion as usual."

"Of course," Fletcher replied.

"I have another appointment so, Robert, if you don't mind seeing Fletcher out for me."

"Sure." Robert watched as Farrah left the conference room.

"A discrepancy in your net worth? Is that the best you could come up with?" Fletcher asked through gritted teeth. "I wouldn't make a mistake like that."

"It was the first thing that popped into my mind," Robert defended, inwardly kicking himself for being so lame.

"She's distracted. She didn't even see through that lie. Anything I can do?" Fletcher asked.

"No, we got it…or we will."

"Good. I know you got a lot going on, but man, you gotta tell her the truth," Fletcher said, walking to the glass door. "And soon. I'll see myself out."

Robert perched on the edge of the conference table and stared out the window as his thoughts went back several weeks to the last time he and Farrah discussed ending their marriage.

Robert stood in the doorway of his master bedroom as he watched Farrah pack her overnight bag. "You said you'd give us time," Robert challenged, trying to keep his voice even.

"I have…we've had months of fun, but it's time to move on."

"Fun…you're saying this has just been fun for you?"

"And you, too," she said, snapping the closure on her bag before moving on to collect her toiletries from the bathroom. "Our whole relationship has been centered on work and sex. Great sex, but that's all."

"That's not true." Robert walked up to Farrah and stared down into her eyes.

Farrah placed her right hand on his chest. "Yes, it is, and that's okay."

"No...it's not," Robert insisted, holding her gaze and using the thumb and index finger of his right hand to capture her chin "We have other common interests and we make each other laugh. Hell, you get the geek in me, and I understand that complex legal mind of yours. We see what's beyond the outside."

Farrah closed her eyes, breaking eye contact. Robert dropped his hand. Farrah slowly opened her eyes again. "This was a game that went way too far. It never was supposed to be anything serious to begin with."

"Look, we can—"

"No." Farrah held up her hand to ward off any further protest. "We need to end this before things get weird and it starts to affect our working relationship."

"Is that what you really want?" he asked, fisting his hands at his sides.

Farrah ignored his question and said, "I think we should have Fletcher handle this for us. He'll take care of everything quickly and quietly."

Robert took that in for a few seconds. "Fine. I'll meet with him tomorrow, but answer my question," he demanded with a little more force in his voice than he'd expected.

Farrah took a step back and removed her wedding band. She placed it on his nightstand and picked up her bag. "It's for the best," she said before walking out the door.

"No, it's not," he said to her retreating back.

"Okay, spill."

Robert turned to find Meeks standing in the doorway of the conference room. "What was that?" Robert asked.

Meeks closed the door behind him and moved toward his best friend. "Spill."

Robert sighed. He could float a lot past most people, but Meeks could nail him dead to rights. "You sure? You want it all this time?"

"You look like you're going to explode if you don't talk to someone. So yeah, tell me everything."

Robert gestured to the chairs that he and Fletcher had once occupied. "We'd better sit. This could take a minute."

"One large white chocolate mocha with extra whipped cream," Paul said, walking into Farrah's office carrying two large coffee mugs while holding his tablet under his arm.

"Thanks. You read my mind."

"You ready to discuss where we are with everything for the baby shower?" Paul asked, excitement written all over his face.

"I'm ready. I have a little time before my meeting with Trey."

Paul sat in the chair across from Farrah's desk. He pulled out his tablet and addressed all the elements of the plans he and Felicia had made for the surprise baby shower they were throwing for Francine. After going through his full checklist, he looked up to find that Farrah hadn't touched her coffee yet and was staring off into space.

"You all right? Something wrong with your coffee?" he asked.

She lowered her gaze. "I'm fine and the coffee's perfect. Sounds like you have everything under control. It's going to be great."

"So you're good with the three male strippers I ordered?"

"Sure," she said, the cup midway to her lips. She frowned and lowered it instantly. "Wait, what?"

Paul slapped his hand on his thigh and almost rolled on the floor, he was laughing so hard. "That's what I thought. You haven't heard a word I've said."

"Sorry, my mind was elsewhere," Farrah said before using her tongue to swipe some whipped cream and taking a sip of her coffee.

"That's obvious," he shot back. "What's going on?"

"I was thinking about Robert and a conversation I just had with Francine."

"Let me guess, she told you to come clean with Robert about your feelings." Paul lifted his cup in mock salute.

"Basically."

"So…"

Farrah smiled, picked up her phone and sent Robert a text. Dinner tonight…my place at seven? She placed her phone on the folders in front of her. Within a minute her phone beeped. Farrah scooped it up, read the text and smiled. "We're having dinner tonight."

"Good, and don't worry about the shower. Between me, Felicia, and the party planner we hired, nothing is going to fall through the cracks. It's going to be perfect, with no crazy surprises," he assured with a great deal of confidence.

"I'm not worried," she said, then asked, "No strippers, right?"

"You just concentrate on that serious conversation you're going to have with Robert tonight."

Farrah's eyes scanned the photos of her parents and Francine's wedding pictures that sat on a small side table in the corner of her office. "I will. I'm done running. Robert's not the playboy that I thought he was. I know in my heart that I can trust him." Farrah went to her safe. Her jewelry box was sitting on top of that large manila envelope Robert had given her that she'd finally gotten around to opening. "And, I have something I need to return."

Chapter 21

"Let me make sure I understand." Meeks scratched his nose. "After you and Farrah wrapped the case in Vegas, you spent a little time playing. You ran into some old college friends of Farrah's and you all gambled together. *You* started losing intentionally, which required you two to complete a dare, which turned out to be that you both had to get married...to each other...which you did."

Robert offered a slow nod. "Yep."

"And because you two...hit it off so well, you decided to stay married a while. Only now Farrah's decided to end it before things get weird. Only because you love her, you lied about getting the divorce she insisted upon," Meeks said, frowning.

"That about sums it up. You know, this really is your fault."

Meeks threw his head back, laughed and clapped once. "My fault...how is any of this my fault?"

"You sent me to help out on that case when we both know if wasn't necessary. You just wanted to keep Francine from going. You were in your 'I'll do anything to keep Francine near me' phase. Well, you got that now, and all you had to do was get married to her and knock her up with your twins."

Both men laughed. "You better not let Francine hear you say that," Meeks warned.

"No, *you* better not let her hear me say that," Robert countered.

"This isn't about us. It's about you and Farrah and how you plan to handle things moving forward."

Robert's phone started dancing across the conference room table. He picked it up, stared at the screen and smiled. "Farrah just pushed our dinner back to eight."

"Good, that'll give you time to figure out what you're going to say. You have to tell her everything, and if I were you, I'd start with how you feel," Meeks suggested.

"You think that'll take the sting out of my lie?"

"Hell, no, this is a Blake sister we're talking about. She'll be pissed regardless, but at least she'll understand why you did it."

"I hope so. I really can't lose her," Robert said, lowering his head slightly.

"So…who is it?"

Farrah looked up from the document she'd been reviewing. "What?"

"Who's the person that's stopping you from having dinner with me?" Trey asked from the doorway.

Farrah groaned. "No one's stopping me from doing anything. I choose not to have dinner or anything else with you because you're possibly the most arrogant man

I've ever met. Not to mention a huge player," Farrah said, tapping her pen against the table.

"I'm not arrogant. I'm confident…and determined." Trey entered Farrah's office, smiling as he took the seat across from her desk. "And I'm not a player. I may be a serial dater, but I don't date more than one woman at a time."

"Really?"

"Yes, really. I have a mother, hell, and two sisters for that matter, and they'd all kick my ass."

Farrah laughed. "Now *that* I believe."

"Now that that's all cleared up, who's got your attention?" He scanned her desk and his gaze landed on a set of drawings. "Wait, let me guess. Mr. Technology himself."

"My personal life's off-limits," she warned. "Besides, what if I'm just not interested?"

"Not possible. Look at me. Add to that, I'm brilliant and just as rich as you," he said, leaning back in his chair.

Farrah dropped her pen and glared at him. "Do you hear yourself?"

"You have to admit, I'd at least garner one date if your mind wasn't already elsewhere."

Farrah rolled her eyes.

"Okay, I'll drop it." Trey raised both hands. "Seriously though, whoever he is, he's a very lucky man. Now as for the response, once you get the affidavit from the forger, you'll be good to go, but you knew that already."

"Indeed."

"Then why go along with this expensive endeavor?" Trey questioned with a scowl. "You knew you hadn't made any errors with your initial filings, and once you find the forger, you'll have all the proof you need to win the case. Nine times out of ten, you wouldn't even have to appear in court," Trey explained.

"I know that, but the board still insisted on a second opinion, so to speak."

"Well, you got the co-signer you needed, and I got a lot of billable hours to babysit the work of a brilliant, beautiful woman. If you don't find your answers, you have some additional options you can explore." Trey stood and stared down at Farrah. "For now, my work here is done."

Farrah stood and extended her hand. "Thank you. Until next time, Mr. Steel."

Trey gifted Farrah with a wide smile, took her hand and kissed the back of it. "Until next time, Ms. Blake."

"Boss, you got a second?" Robert's assistant, Jeremy, asked as he entered the office holding his iPad.

Robert looked up from his computer. "What's up?"

"We ran a trace on that bank account number you got from Butch Johnson and something strange popped up," Jeremy said, removing his glasses and placing them on his head, concealing them in his curly black hair.

"What?"

Jeremy's six-foot form hovered in front of Robert's desk as he explained. "The number was tied to one of our company's old inactive accounts. I mean really old accounts, like from several years ago when Ted Jefferson worked here. This means someone from the inside had to work this out," he handed Robert his iPad.

Robert looked down at the screen and frowned. "So are you thinking Junior and his father are behind all this?"

"That I don't know. What I *do* know is there hasn't been any activity on this account in years, and this transaction took place long after Senior was dead," Jeremy explained.

Robert sat with his right hand over his mouth and gave Jeremy a slow nod.

"Someone could be using the Jeffersons to do their dirty work," Jeremy offered.

Robert lowered his hand to his desk. "Junior did say he didn't find out about any of this until someone brought it to his attention."

"Who?"

"I don't know. Junior won't say. He was basically *told* that it was his father's last wish for him to seek acknowledgment and compensation for Senior's so-called designs. Designs Junior actually believes we stole from his father. Designs that he wasn't even capable of creating, according to Farrah's father."

"So he could be a victim in this, too? But who's pulling his strings?" Jeremy asked.

Robert shrugged. "Maybe this Ruby Lee—or should I say, Lee Rugby—can help us answer that question."

"Yeah, about that?"

"What about it?" Robert asked, his confusion clear.

"I know Alexia Gray told Farrah to look for information in her files under Lee Rugby, but everything we found led to a dead end. The burner cell phone numbers, bank accounts connected to shell companies that transferred money to accounts in the Virgin Islands, and several grainy surveillance photos." Jeremy scratched his head.

"Send the pictures down to the lab for processing. Let's see what they can come up with."

"Yes, sir." Jeremy turned to leave, only to halt his progress. He turned and said, "I hate to say it, boss, but this is more sophisticated than anything that Alexia could pull off on her own."

"I agree." Robert cracked his knuckles. "I put the name Lee Rugby through every database you can think of, and even a few you aren't aware of, and there's nothing. It's like this person doesn't even...*exist*."

Jeremy's brown eyes widened. "You think Alexia lied? That she knows more than what she's sharing or she's even holding something back?"

"No, she wouldn't take a chance on anything happening to that Blige girl. She gave us everything she had. What I think is that she might be being used, too, but doesn't realize it."

"By who?"

"That's the million-dollar question. I think I know who can help us figure it out," Robert said with a grin. "Get Charles in here. I need him and his team to make a quick trip."

Chapter 22

Farrah stood in the middle of her kitchen, surveying her completed dinner. "The fettuccine Alfredo is ready, the jumbo shrimp and spinach is perfect and the wine is chilling. Nice job, girl," she said just as there was a knock on the door. Farrah glanced at the hall mirror to make sure her blue formfitting scoop-neck dress was sending the sexy message she wanted. Feeling so confident that she was even wearing her big black-and-white dice slippers, Farrah opened her door and released a small gasp at the sight of the man standing before her.

Robert stood with his hands in the pockets of a pair of black jeans. He wore a simple black T-shirt covered by a black leather jacket and black combat boots—a combination he only wore when he was riding on his Harley, another one of his favorite toys. Farrah's eyes roamed his body and a slow, sexy smile spread across her face. "Good evening," she said.

"Good evening." Robert looked down at her feet and shook his head. "I see you still have the big dice slippers I bought you in Vegas."

Farrah wiggled her feet. "Of course. They were a wedding present…sort of, remember?"

Robert smirked. "They came with our wedding package. How I could forget?"

"Come in," she said, stepping aside and gesturing for him to enter.

Robert walked in, smiled and gave his head a small shake. "It's like walking into a jewelry box whenever I come to your place."

Farrah gave him a playful shove, but she knew her midcentury-meets-old-school-glamour taste in furnishing was over-the-top, but she didn't care. She loved the light gray tufted sofa and matching wingback chairs, the uniquely designed Italian crystal light fixtures throughout her place that Robert loved to make fun of. And she especially liked the expensive three- and four-dimensional paintings that found homes on several of her cream-colored walls.

"Whatever, at least my place can't be mistaken for an expensive sports bar. Would you like something to drink?" Farrah asked, retrieving the bottle of Stella Rosa from the ice bucket sitting on her kitchen counter.

"Sure."

Farrah filled two wineglasses and handed one to Robert. "Cheers," she said, raising her glass. Farrah placed the bottle on the bar in front of Robert.

"Cheers," he echoed. Robert gazed at Farrah over the rim of his glass.

His gaze sent a warm chill down Farrah's spine. She turned, breaking the connection, and retrieved two plates from the cabinet. "I hope you're hungry," she said, sliding the creamy pasta on the plate before adding a generous amount of shrimp and spinach.

"I'm starving," he said, leering as he took another drink from his glass. "I know people aren't allowed to eat in your living room and your dining area seems too formal, so do you mind if we eat here at the bar? I know you paid a fortune for this—and it's beautiful, by the way. But we might as well make good use of it," he added, indicating her red-enameled lava countertop.

"Thank you, and of course we can." Farrah handed Robert his plate and when their fingers met, their gazes collided and her body tingled. She joined Robert at the bar and nudged him a little. "You remember the Blake rule, don't you? I cooked, so you clean."

Robert laughed. "Deal," he replied as he leaned over and kissed her on the corner of the mouth. Their eyes held for a moment, but before Farrah could react, Robert righted himself and began to eat his food.

Unlike during their last meal, their conversation now did finally shift to the case and what they were doing to find Ruby Lee. "Farrah, we're going to find whoever it is that started this whole mess," Robert promised.

"I know we will."

Robert picked up the wine bottle. "More wine?"

"No, I'm good, thanks."

"Do you also know…well, understand anyway, why I wanted an outsider to handle the case from this point?" Robert asked, his forehead creased and eyes slightly narrowed.

Farrah saw something in his eyes that she hadn't before—concern. And it touched her heart. "I think I finally get it."

Robert released a breath and the worry she once saw was replaced by a look of relief. "I was only trying to protect you, your career. You're the lead attorney defending a case against your family's security company for fraud against a thief with millions of dollars at risk. If this thing goes sideways, I didn't want your name attached."

Farrah placed her fork across the top of her plate. "Why didn't you just talk to me about your concerns?"

"And what would you have said?" Robert asked.

"To mind your business and that I can take care of myself and my career."

"Exactly," he countered. "Which is why I went to the board to get the help I knew I'd need to convince you to see things my way. Think about it. Even the hint of anything improper could do irreparable damage to your career, especially in this industry."

Farrah took a slow sip of her wine. "I get it," she admitted on a weary sigh.

"Good, now can I have some more of that outstanding fettuccine?" he asked, sliding his plate in her direction.

"Sure, help yourself," she said, smiling as she slid his plate back to him.

Robert chuckled, heading into the kitchen with plate in hand.

Robert refilled their glasses with the last of the contents of that deliciously sweet Moscato before tossing it into her recycle bin. "I didn't see another one in the fridge. Should I pull one out of that wine vault of yours?"

"It's not a vault. And there's another bottle chilling in the wine bar," she instructed. "I figured you'd need more after cleaning the kitchen. Nice job, by the way. Not many men would bypass the dishwasher in favor of doing them by hand."

"Well, Momma Penny made sure her only son could take care of himself no matter what. There were only a handful of dishes to wash. Besides, I don't think you've ever used that industrial dishwasher of yours, so it didn't seem right that I'd be the first to break it in. I'm just happy there really were dishes to wash."

"What's that supposed to mean?" she asked, finishing off the last of her wine.

"I just knew I'd find empty boxes in here…you know, from wherever you bought that delicious dinner from."

Farrah leaned back in her chair and laughed so hard she tipped back. Robert was around the bar so fast she didn't even realize she was about to hit the floor. "Thanks," Farrah said in a voice barely above a whisper.

Robert stared into Farrah's eyes. There, he saw his own need and desire reflected back at him. Male instincts wanted control…wanted to devour her whole, but Robert didn't want to simply satisfy an animalistic need. They had something that deserved to be nurtured in a way that a couple in love should. Farrah deserved to be cherished and Robert intended to do just that. He picked her up and carried her through the living room and down the hall to the master bedroom. He placed her gently on the bed and kneeled before her. Farrah held his gaze but remained silent, but by the heated look in her eyes and rise and fall of her breasts, Robert knew she wanted him as much as he wanted her.

Robert cupped Farrah's face in the palms of his hands, where he began to kiss her, first lightly on her nose, then her right cheek, followed by the corner of her mouth. He raised his head, stared into her eyes and said, "I'm done waiting. I'm crazy about you and I want my woman back."

Farrah stared into his eyes and matched Robert's move by taking his face in her hands. "I'm back," she said before kissing him passionately on the lips. "I'm crazy about you, too."

"We should talk—"

"Later. Much, much later," Farrah said as she stood and stepped away from him.

Robert turned to follow Farrah's retreating form. "Where…"

Farrah paused and then turned to face him. She reached behind her back and unzipped her dress, letting it fall to the floor. Farrah stood before Robert in her black strapless bra and matching lace panties. "Damn, you're beautiful," Robert said, rising to his feet, his sex hard as steel. He walked over to Farrah and his eyes took their fill. "I adore you, baby."

"Prove it," she challenged.

Robert was undressed and standing naked before Farrah within a matter of seconds. He swept her off her feet and carried her back to the bed where he placed her in its center. "I think I'm overdressed," she said, rising up on her elbows.

"You won't be for long."

Farrah smiled and lay back down. Robert's manhood throbbed as he fought the urge to take her as she lay open before him. He reminded himself that this night was about pleasing Farrah. Showing her how much he loved her both in and out of bed, even though he hadn't said the words yet. Robert kissed his way up Farrah's leg, letting his nose and lips enjoy the soft, silky skin of her thighs. He slowly removed her lace panties, tossing them to the side. Robert kissed her core in a way that had her hips rising off the bed. He used his fingers to assist him in his efforts, sending Farrah over the edge, screaming out his name.

"Damn," Farrah moaned.

"We've only just begun, baby." Robert rolled Farrah onto her stomach, unlatched her bra and sent it to join the discarded panties on the floor. He pulled her up by her hips, bringing her to her knees. He pressed his body against her back. He brushed her hair to one side and kissed the back of her neck. Robert kissed, licked and nibbled his way down her shoulder. He used his hands to explore her body, her breasts, stomach, and finally her sex. The fingers of his right hand pushed Farrah to her erotic edge, causing her to scream out his name yet again.

Farrah fell forward back onto her stomach and tried to catch her breath as Robert's hands and lips roamed her back and butt. She rolled onto her back and rewarded Robert with a satisfied sigh. "You've worked hard enough, don't you think?" she asked, summoning him with her right index finger.

"Making love to you isn't work, baby, it's pure pleasure," Robert said, his voice every bit as husky. He hovered over Farrah for several moments before kissing her until they both were gasping for air.

"Well, it's time we both experienced the pleasure," she said, parting her thighs for him.

Robert kissed Farrah as he slowly entered her, enjoying every sensation his body was experiencing. While he'd made love to Farrah a number of times before, this night was special, in spite of the secret that he had yet to confess. Their bodies set a pace that had them both reaching peaks and valleys of pleasure that only they could provide each other.

"Baby, you're amazing," Robert whispered while stroking her hair.

"So are you." Farrah kissed his chest before she rolled from on top of him and left the bed.

"Where are you going?" Robert asked while reaching for her.

Farrah giggled as she dodged his hands. "I'm going to get the shower ready. Care to join me?"

Robert rolled to his side, resting his face on his right hand. "Of course I would."

"Can you go get another bottle of wine? I have a feeling we're going to want it soon," Farrah said, laughing as she entered the bathroom.

Robert walked naked into the kitchen and retrieved the wine, a corkscrew and two glasses. On his way back to the bedroom, he noticed a manila envelope that he recognized immediately lying on the edge of her end table. "Damn!" Robert felt as though he'd just been hit in the gut. Meeks's words popped into his mind. *This is a Blake sister we're talking about. She'll be pissed, but at least she'll understand why you did it.*

"Robert, you get lost?" Farrah called from the bathroom.

"I'm on my way, sweetheart," Robert replied, staring at the unopened envelope, and whispered, "I hope you're right, man."

Chapter 23

"Mmm," Farrah moaned as her eyes slowly opened, greeting the morning sun shining through sheer drapes covering her wall of windows. She smiled as memories of last night's activities flooded her mind. Farrah rolled onto her back, prepared to wake Robert in the same manner he'd woken her only a few hours earlier. Instead of finding his sleeping form lying next to her, she found a note on his pillow. A shiver of disappointment cycled through her body as Farrah sprang forward and grabbed the note.

Enjoy your coffee. Had to go into the office and I didn't want to wake you. See you later, baby.

Within seconds of reading the note, Farrah's senses were assaulted by the aroma of fresh-brewed coffee, her favorite vanilla roast that she knew she'd been out of.

"Nice move, Robert, going out and getting my coffee," she said, placing the note on the nightstand.

Farrah slipped into a silk robe and made her way to her kitchen. Before she could cross the threshold from the hall into the open-concept living area, she was met by a large crystal vase with a dozen long-stemmed black roses—her favorites—sitting on the side table in her foyer. A wide smile spread across Farrah's face as she walked, giggling, toward the beautiful bouquet. She reached for the card and read it out loud. "I really liked that thing you did on that funny-looking baby sofa in your bedroom." Farrah shook her head. "It's a chaise," she corrected, though he wasn't around to hear it.

Farrah inhaled the wonderful scent of the roses before going into her kitchen. A large cup was sitting next to a full pot of coffee. She poured herself a cup, opened the refrigerator to retrieve the creamer, only to find a platter of fresh-cut fruit and another note. Farrah reached for the note and stood in front of the open refrigerator as she read it out loud, too. "I adore you and I can't wait to show and tell you how much in person."

Farrah could feel the tears as they began to well in her eyes. While Robert hadn't told her that he loved her yet, his actions lately most certainly had. Farrah wiped away the single tear that escaped before reaching for the creamer. She added two teaspoons to her coffee and returned the bottle to the refrigerator. Farrah selected a tiny chunk of pineapple from the plate and popped it in her mouth, then took a seat at her bar. She turned on her iPad, propped it up and dialed her sister. She enjoyed several sips of coffee while waiting for her call to connect.

"Good morning, sis," Farrah said to the half-awake reflection of herself.

"Good *night* would be more appropriate," Felicia replied, sitting up in her bed and adjusting her superhero pajama top.

"You still asleep?"

Felicia frowned. "Still? Farrah, there's a fourteen-hour time difference. It's ten o'clock and I've been up for thirteen hours. Whatever it is couldn't wait?"

"Sorry, I keep forgetting. I guess it could wait," Farrah said.

"No, I'm up now," Felicia said in a dry tone. "What's going on?"

Farrah took another sip of her coffee. "Have you seen Fletcher's email?"

"Yes, we finished things up early so I'll be flying to Atlanta in a couple of days."

"You need me to join you?"

"No, I'm good," Felicia reassured.

"You know not to sign off on any papers until I see them, right?" Farrah reminded, her eyebrows shooting up.

"Yes, of course. Now since you got me up, tell me what's going on between you and Robert. I hear you're finally dealing with your feelings for the man," she asked, adjusting the pillow behind her.

"Who was it, Francine or Paul?"

"Both actually, but that's beside the point."

"Not really," Farrah said, sighing at the thought of the two people she was going to have a long talk with.

"So…" Felicia pushed a wayward piece of hair from her face. "What's going on? By the look of those beautiful roses in the background, things must be pretty darn good. He knows how much you like a unique flower. That's a good sign…so let's hear it, and don't leave out any details."

"You mean your triplet radar is off, too?" Farrah asked, laughing.

"Yes, I think Francine's twins are interfering with our connection."

"Thank goodness." Farrah took a quick sip of her coffee. "It can be quite inconvenient at times."

"Stop avoiding the question and spill before I fall asleep," Felicia demanded, yawning.

"There's just so much more to Robert than I ever realized. We all know he's gorgeous, brilliant, and can make a woman—"

"TMI, sis. TMI."

"Sorry," she said, offering Felicia a sheepish grin. "Robert's not that same playboy we met five years ago. The way he loves and protects his mother reminds me of how we feel about our parents. You should see them together…it's so sweet. Did you know he designed and built her a house? Of course not, he's so private about everything," Farrah said, shaking her head.

"Wow…"

"What?" Farrah asked, frowning.

"Francine was right. You're in love. Have you told him yet?"

Farrah's shoulders dropped and she lowered her head slightly. "Not yet. I was going to last night before we got…distracted. Anyway, he hasn't said anything yet, either."

"But you know he does, right?" Felicia asked, the concern in her voice mirrored her facial expression.

"I think so…yes, I know he does," Farrah said, nodding slowly.

"Good. I'm happy for you. Both of you."

"So, you still keeping men at arm's length?" Farrah asked with her left eyebrow raised.

"Not intentionally. I'm just busy, not to mention I've been on the other side of the world for the last year. Besides, most men don't want to deal with a nerdy, twenty-eight-year-old virgin," she said, slumping down in the bed.

"First off, you're a successful, brilliant doctor doing top-secret research crap for the CIA. Something that doesn't have to do with men's inability to get it up."

Felicia burst into laughter.

"Second," Farrah continued. "Your virginal status is by choice. It's not like you're holding out for marriage or anything. Are you? Not that there's anything wrong with that."

"No, it's just never happened for me." Felicia sank lower in the bed. "And at the rate I'm going, I'm going to be a successful, brilliant spinster."

"Don't be ridiculous," Farrah chided. "As soon as you take care of this will business, we'll work on getting you some business."

Felicia covered her face with her pillow and laughed. "On that crazy note, I'm going to bed."

"Well, at least you have the right idea."

"Shut up, Farrah. I'll call when I get to Atlanta."

"Okay, good night. Love you," Farrah said, smiling.

"Good morning and I love you more," Felicia replied before ending the call.

Farrah closed her iPad, freshened up her coffee, grabbed a few more pieces of fruit and headed to her bathroom. She placed her cup on the counter, pulled her hair up and turned on the shower. Farrah stepped under the spray and began washing away the evidence of last night's and this morning's activities when Felicia's words came back to her. *He knows how much you like unique flowers.* Yes, he truly did. It was a remark that jarred a long-buried memory.

"Good morning, Ms. Blake," Ms. Ruthie, the sisters' temporary assistant, greeted.

"Good morning," Farrah replied, accepting the mes-

sages the older woman held out. "Oh, my, I just love those flowers. Are they yours?"

"Yes," she replied, smiling.

"Gift from your husband...children?" Farrah asked.

"I don't have any children," she replied, breaking eye contact and putting her attention on the bright pink bouquet. "My husband sent them to me. It's the anniversary of when we first met."

"That's so sweet," Farrah said as she flipped through her messages.

"Thank you. I know this is the last day I'm covering Paul's desk, but I couldn't stand to be apart from them. My husband had to go through a lot of trouble to get them for me. I tried to tell him it wasn't necessary, but he insisted."

"I don't blame you," Farrah said as she examined the bouquet. "They're beautiful and different. Do you mind my asking what kind they are?"

"Not at all," she replied, taking one of them from the base. "They're actually from a plant that blooms in late summer, so they had to be special-ordered and flown in. It's called Ruby Spice, although my husband calls it the Ruby Lee...after me," she proudly explained.

Farrah's hold on the soap failed and it landed on the porcelain with a solid thud. "Oh, my God... Ruby Lee."

Chapter 24

Robert walked into the gray, windowless concrete room that the team often used for information-gathering sessions, as he called them, to find a rumple-shirted, blue-jeans-wearing Butch Johnson pacing the room. The man stopped long enough to acknowledge Robert's presence and glare at Charles, the tall, stocky, caramel-skinned senior agent Robert had assigned to retrieve Butch from that sordid little spot in New Orleans and bring him to their offices.

"Thank you for accepting the invitation to join us. This shouldn't take long. The sooner you answer my questions, the faster we'll be able to get you back to the Big Easy," Robert explained, wanting to wrap this all up in the next few minutes. Robert didn't want to go another day without telling Farrah the truth about everything, including the fact that he loved her.

Butch stopped in his tracks and stood facing Robert

with his arms folded. "Invitation," he taunted, slanting his head slightly. He shot an accusatory glare to Charles and pointed at him. "That body builder wannabe wearing your uniform showed up to my place and told me I had five minutes to get into his vehicle or he'd handcuff me and drag me out by my hair," he said, dropping his arms. "I've been stuck in this godforsaken room for nearly twelve hours. Does that sound like a damn invitation to you?"

Robert turned and faced Charles. "Really?"

"What?" Charles shrugged. "You told me to get here right away, no matter what."

"I meant to offer him a payment for his time," Robert explained.

Meeks entered the room just in time to hear Butch's complaint and Robert's response. "I see you have everything under control as usual," he said, leaning back against the door.

"Somebody said something about money?" Butch spoke up, his anger seeming to dissipate.

Charles looked at both Robert and Meeks. "He's had bathroom breaks and he's been fed," he explained.

Robert turned back toward Butch and gestured to the chair across from the door. "Have a seat."

"I'm fine, thanks," he said, standing again with his arms folded over a bulky chest. "What's this about money?"

"I apologize for the confusion. We'll reimburse you for your time and inconvenience. Please sit." Robert once again gestured toward the chair.

"I'm cool," he said, waving off the request.

"When we were in New Orleans, you told us you were the middle man for Ruby Lee."

"Yeah, that's right," Butch said.

"What you failed to tell us was that Ruby Lee doesn't really exist," Robert said.

Butch's eyes widened slightly. "I don't know what you're talking about," he insisted.

"Oh, but I think you do," Robert countered, cornering the table and moving past Charles until he stood in front of Butch. He was trying hard to keep his anger under control. "Ruby Lee isn't in anybody's database or on anybody's radar. And that account number you gave us led to one of our very own accounts."

"Maybe Ruby Lee worked for your company like Alexia did," Butch replied, not bothering to keep the sarcasm from his voice.

Meeks frowned at the suggestion but remained silent.

"Did you not hear the man?" Charles asked, scowling at Butch. "Ruby Lee doesn't exist."

"I think I'll take that seat after all," Butch said, pulling out the chair and sitting down. Robert sat on the edge of the table in front of him.

Their guest sighed. "Look, all I know is someone calling themselves Ruby Lee contacted me about the job and putting them together with Alexia. They wired me two hundred and fifty thousand dollars to make the connection and from that point on, Alexia handled the specifics of the job with Ruby Lee directly."

"Two hundred and fifty thousand dollars," Charles said, shaking his head, his disbelief clear. "…for a connection?"

"And the forger, how did she connect with whoever did the work?" Meeks asked.

Butch hesitated before saying, "I…I don't know."

Robert leaned forward and stared into Butch's eyes. "I'm losing my patience…and when I lose my patience,

Charles loses his. When that happens, things won't work out well for you. Who's the forger?"

"I swear I don't know who she used," he insisted. "She rejected everybody I tried to set her up with. She thought I was an idiot for thinking any of the people I offered up were any good. She said she'd take care of it. Apparently she has her own people."

"Her own forger?" Robert replied, looking back at Meeks.

"What did she mean by that?" Charles asked, moving closer to the table.

"I don't know," Butch shrugged. "I just assumed she already had someone."

"Did you ever meet this Ruby Lee in person?" Robert asked.

"Just once, to get Alexia's final payment."

"Can you describe her?" Meeks asked, crossing his arms.

"Not really. She wore a baseball hat, sunglasses, and she had a really great body."

"Wonderful. That can be anybody," Robert grumbled, rubbing his face with the back of his hand.

"Do you remember what she drove…a plate number perhaps?" Meeks inquired.

Butch smirked. "Yeah, a new red Mercedes, and the letters on the temporary plates were *R-E-D*."

"How can you be so sure?" Robert asked, with a puckered brow.

"Because I remember thinking how funny it was that a curly-haired redhead was driving a red car with the letters *R-E-D* on the plates," Butch explained, grinning.

"What?" Meeks snapped, pushing himself off the door.

Robert turned to face him. "That has to be a coincidence."

* * *

Farrah entered her office to find Francine staring out the window, waiting for her. Her sister looked really sleek in a sleeveless deep green maternity dress that brought out the green in her eyes. "Good, you're here." For a minute, Farrah felt underdressed, wearing their company's standard uniform. "You know, we really should have had a maternity uniform made for you."

"Funny. Very funny. You said it was important. What's up?"

"You look great, by the way."

"Now who's being a comedian?" Francine shot back.

"Have a seat," Farrah said, gesturing to one of the chairs across from her desk.

Francine sat down and Farrah took the chair beside her. "What's going on, sis? Did something happen between you and Robert?"

In spite of the news she was about to share, Farrah couldn't help the smile that spread across her face. "Yes, but that's not what this is about," she replied.

"Then what is this about?"

"Do you remember when we first joined the firm? You were an agent and I was fresh out of law school," Farrah reminded.

"Of course I do. Daddy was both proud and scared."

They shared a laugh.

"Yes, he was," Farrah nodded. "Remember when we had that floating admin pool and everyone's assistant had to cover for each other?"

"Yeah, Paul hated that, too. Why?"

"There was a lady about mom's age, shoulder-length sandy hair. Her name was Ruthie Lee Rutherford. Remember her?"

Francine's gaze narrowed on her sister. "Vaguely, why?"

"I think she might be our Ruby Lee aka Lee Rugby."

Francine's eyes widened. "What?"

"I think, somehow, some way, she's connected to all of this."

Francine gave a dismissive wave. "No way. I'm sure Butch Johnson would have noticed if he was dealing with an older woman. He certainly would have told us that, too."

"You didn't meet him. I have a feeling he wouldn't give up anything over the bare minimum. Besides, Alexia said Ruby Lee didn't have anything we could hold over her. Maybe that's because she's older and doesn't have anyone."

"Everyone has someone," Francine insisted.

"Ms. Ruthie didn't have any children. Although, she does have a husband…or at least she did."

"Who has a husband?" Paul asked as he walked into the office holding three coffee mugs. "Two coffees and one hot chocolate."

"Perfect timing," Farrah said, accepting the cup he held out to her. "Paul, do you remember Ruthie Lee Rutherford? She was an assistant in that temporary pool we had about five years ago."

"Yeah, I remember Ms. Ruthie." Paul blew into his coffee. "Poor thing. But I think you're wrong. She never had a husband."

"What? Why do you say that?" Farrah asked, looking up at him. "She told me she had a husband. He sent her flowers. I saw them."

"I know. We all saw the flowers and gifts, but they weren't from her husband. That's just what she told everyone. She was a little off, but it had to be hell being someone's mistress for over twenty years, only to have him die on you," Paul said before taking a sip of his coffee as he leaned against Farrah's desk. "Although rumor has it he left her pretty well off. Too bad she can't really enjoy it."

Farrah and Francine shared a questioning look before turning their glares on Paul.

"What?" Farrah asked.

Paul placed his cup on the desk, then looked at both women. "You two really don't know?"

Both women shook their heads.

"Ruthie Lee Rutherford was the longtime mistress of former executive…turned board member…turned vendor…wait for it…Ted Jefferson."

"Ted Jefferson!" Farrah leaned forward and placed her cup on the desk next to Paul's. "The same Ted Jefferson that's suing us?"

"Actually it's his son who's suing us," Francine clarified.

Farrah glared at her sister. "Semantics."

"Yep," Paul said, shaking his head. "The same Ted Jefferson who embezzled money and tried to steal plans for several of our new security systems to cover his gambling debts."

"*That's* why we fired him. Dad would never say why, not even when Ted died. He wouldn't even discuss it when his son filed this ridiculous suit. He said it was irrelevant," Francine added.

"Irrelevant… How can he being a thief be irrelevant?"

Francine shrugged. "You know what Dad says. Forgiven misdeeds should be left in the past."

"And if I remember correctly, Ruthie Lee Rutherford left the company right after he did," Farrah confirmed.

"Yep," Paul replied.

"Hell, if she thought her man was treated unfairly, she might want some type of revenge against the company," Farrah stated.

"Wait… Your Dad got him help, and he repaid every dime he stole."

"That must be why there's no record of him ever being arrested. Dad made sure the board never pressed charges," Francine theorized, taking a healthy sip of her hot chocolate.

"He also cleaned up his act and went on to build a successful construction company," Paul confirmed.

"If I remember correctly, we did business with him for years until he got sick and passed," Francine offered. "What do either of them have to do with any of this?"

"I don't know. What I do know is that a slightly eccentric Ruthie Lee Rutherford, a woman that had a great deal of access when she was here and could've had a motive to want to do her former lover's company harm, told me that her *husband* called her Ruby Lee after her favorite flower." Farrah held up her right hand and hunched her shoulders. "Now, that can't be a coincidence, and I think it's worth checking into."

Chapter 25

"There's no way she could have had anything to do with any of this," Robert said, pulling out his cell to send the incoming call to voice mail. "She's behind bars and that's where she'll stay."

"Who are you talking about?" Charles asked.

"A crazy old girlfriend of Meeks's," Robert replied.

"Jasmine Black," Meeks said, his face twisted as though he was in pain. "Her obsession for me took it to a whole new level of crazy. From bailing out and buying a gun for someone we'd just put away so he could kill Francine to infiltrating our company to keep tabs on us, and from hiding behind and controlling stalkers to actually trying to kill Francine herself."

After Jasmine's attempts were foiled, she'd been sent to jail and was currently awaiting trial.

"We both know how resourceful she can be, not to mention vengeful. She could have easily coordinated something like this," Meeks insisted, pacing the room.

"But whoever pulled this off had to have been planning this for quite some time, long before Jasmine ever came on the scene." Robert reached to stop his friend's movements. "Think about it. They planted someone in our organization to steal that info, and then planted bogus documents that would guarantee we'd lose the lawsuit, costing us millions. Their motive had to be something pretty significant. No offense, Meeks, but wanting you back in her life and her bed just doesn't seem like it's a big enough reason."

"I agree," Charles echoed. "No offense." He held up both hands.

"I know she's diabolical, but this is a bit much even for Jasmine…even to have you," Robert added.

"I hear you," Meeks stated, pacing the room again. "But my gut is telling me that Jasmine is somehow mixed up in all this."

"I know, but…it's a reach," Robert said.

Meeks turned back to Butch. "When she delivered that last payment, did you talk to her?"

"Yeah, why?" he replied, frowning.

"Did she happen to speak with a Southern accent?" Robert asked.

Robert and Meeks held their breath as though their life depended on the next word out of Butch's mouth. "Yeah, she did."

"Okay, say you're right," Francine asked. "Say that this Ruthie Lee Rutherford is really Ruby Lee, aka Lee Rugby. What's her motive for doing any of this?"

"I'm wondering the same thing myself," Paul asked.

"I don't know. Maybe she got pissed off when Dad booted her man out of the company. She might not have seen it as a way to help him." Farrah got up, circled her desk and sat down. "It did take a while for him to get it together. She might have thought Dad and the company had abandoned him when he needed them the most. Who knows? All I'm saying is that we need to check her out." Farrah turned on her computer and logged on to her system. "If someone went after my man, I'd do everything in my power to make things right."

Francine and Paul looked at each other and smiled. "We know you would," Francine teased.

Farrah glared at them before turning her attention back to the screen.

Paul took the seat she'd vacated. "What are you doing?"

"I'm running a quick background check and credit report for Ruthie Lee Rutherford. I want to see what she's been up to all these years."

"What's the plan?" Paul questioned.

"I'm going to find out as much as I can about her, bring Robert up to speed and we'll go pay her a friendly visit." Farrah clicked a few keys on her computer, navigating between multiple search engines and websites dedicated to the types of investigation she needed.

"I think the only thing you're going to find is a sweet, if somewhat sad, little old lady living without the love of her life." Paul stretched out his legs and crossed them at his ankles.

"Farrah, I know you're going to do what you think is best, but I think you're barking up the wrong tree." Francine reached for Paul's hand. "Help me up."

Paul quickly obliged.

"Where are you going?" Farrah asked.

"We're interviewing night nannies. I'm sure you and Robert can handle this, but if not, let us know." Francine kissed Paul on the cheek and blew Farrah a kiss before walking out of the office.

"What now?" Paul asked, returning to his seat and reaching for the stress ball that sat on the edge of Farrah's desk.

"Now we wait," Farrah explained, leaning back in her chair.

"While we wait, care to tell me how your night went?" Paul asked, making his eyebrows dance.

Farrah smiled and released a slow breath.

"That good, huh?" Paul returned the stress ball to the desk. "I guess you won't be needing this anymore."

Farrah giggled.

"Did you two finally confess your undying love for each other yet?"

"Not yet."

"What the hell are you waiting for?" he shot back. "Please don't tell me that you—Ms. I Passed the Bar on the First Try, I Can Kick Butt Just as Good as Any Man and I Shoot Guns for the Fun of It—are still scared."

"I just haven't had the chance…" Farrah started to explain when her computer signaled that the first report had come through. She browsed the report and as the words sank in, realization began to take hold. Farrah felt as though she'd been hit in the gut.

"Well, what's—?"

Farrah held up her index finger and Paul's voice trailed to a halt. He sat quietly, watching as Farrah read through the documents as several others were fed to her screen. She sent the reports to her printer and sat back into her chair.

"Well?" Paul asked again, sitting on the edge of his seat.

Farrah snatched several papers from the printer and

handed them to him. She gave him a few moments to catch up.

"I knew it... Oh, no... Oh, my..."

"*Oh, my* is right."

Paul ran his hands down his face a couple of times. "Are you sure this is correct? Is there any chance that it could be wrong?"

"We have access to some of the best networks in the world, you know that. Plus, I called in a favor from one of Felicia's friends at the CIA. It's right." She tapped the edge of the third page. "Did you see the attachment?"

"Yeah, I saw it. I just don't understand how this is even possible. What are you going to do?"

"Where's Robert?" she asked, trying to keep her emotions in check.

"He's downstairs with Meeks in interrogation."

"Interrogation... Why?" she asked, glancing back down at the papers she still held.

"It *is* called interrogation, so I'd assume they're..."

"Yes but my question is, who's in there with them?" she asked, frowning.

"I have no idea," Paul said. "Jeremy just said Robert had whoever it is flown in last night. Charles and his team brought him up after midnight."

Farrah got to her feet, picked up the reports and headed to the door. "Are you going to tell Francine?"

"Not yet," she replied. "I want to talk to Robert and Meeks first."

"No worries. My lips are sealed where Francine's concerned." He pretended to close an imaginary zipper across his lips. "Looks like you might have been right after all," Paul admitted.

Farrah slowly nodded. "That makes two of us."

Chapter 26

"All right, I admit that seems suspect, but I still really think it's a leap," Robert said.

"What's a leap?" Farrah asked, walking into the interrogation room and coming to a complete halt when a familiar figure in the chair focused an angry glare her way. "And why did you bring Butch Johnson here?"

The rest of the men in the room turned to meet a surprised-looking Farrah. Robert rushed forward, grabbed Farrah's hand and pulled her to his side. It was a move that she happily complied with and one that didn't seem to bother Meeks or Charles.

"That's what I've been trying to figure out for the last fifteen hours," Butch complained, his raspy voice laced with anger again.

"We needed to clear up some additional concerns we had," Meeks said, checking his watch. "Unfortunately I can't stay. We can finish this in about an hour. I have to get upstairs. Francine's expecting me."

Farrah threw up her free hand to stop his advancement. "I know. But I think you need to hear this."

"It can't wait?" Meeks questioned.

"What's going on?" Robert asked, frowning down at her.

Farrah looked at both men. "No."

"All right," Meeks said, but quickly pulled out his cell phone and clicked a few keys. "What is it?"

"I've figured out who's behind all this," she declared.

"That's funny. So have they," Butch chimed in.

Charles gave Butch Johnson the evil eye. "What do you want me to do with Big Mouth here?" he asked, shifting his gaze to Robert.

Robert felt Farrah squeeze his hand. He pushed out a breath and said, "Make him comfortable."

"I'd be very comfortable back home," he replied, taking a few steps toward the door before stopping. "About that money you mentioned." His eyes scanned the men in the room.

"We'll get you back to New Orleans as soon as we can with a little something in your pockets for your *inconvenience*, but in the meantime, please enjoy our hospitality in one of our empty apartments," Robert offered.

"Now you're talking…you got any beer?" Butch asked, following Charles out of the room.

"What did he mean, you two figured out who's behind all this?" Farrah asked, passing a glance between Robert and Meeks.

"You first," Robert insisted.

Everyone took a seat at the table and Farrah shared what she remembered and explained her theory. She had just gotten to the point where she was about to reveal the results of the background check when the door opened.

"What's going on? I understand you have the results of Ms. Ruthie's background check," Francine stated as she entered the room.

Meeks went to his wife's side and helped her into the only vacant chair.

"How do you know that?" Farrah asked.

"I went looking for you, sister dear, after I got Meeks's text telling me to start the interview without him. So I asked Paul where you were," she said to Farrah. "When he did that avoidance thing he does by pretending his lips are sealed, I knew then something was up." Francine looked up at Meeks. "There's no way you'd let me interview any of our nannies without you. So spill…what's going on?"

"It seems the guys think they, too, may know who's behind all this craziness," Farrah explained.

"And Farrah was just about to share the results of her search," Meeks added.

"Well, let's hear it. Somebody say something," Francine said, her eyes skimming the room.

"Baby, you okay?" Meeks asked, reaching over to rub her stomach.

"I'm fine. Our children are just trying to get my attention," Francine reassured Meeks.

Robert brought Farrah's hand to his lips and gently kissed the back of it. Their eyes met and her gaze held him captive. Robert knew the next few moments would be difficult, no matter which theory was correct. He wanted Farrah to know that no matter what, he was there for her and that they'd get through whatever came next together. Farrah lowered her gaze and gave him a single nod.

Francine turned her attention to Farrah. "All right, sis, tell us what you've figured out."

* * *

Farrah leaned forward slightly. "I know you and Paul thought I was reaching with my theory. Secretly, I was afraid I might have been, too. That I could be looking for any reason to clear our name." She squeezed Robert's hand. Farrah could almost feel Robert willing her some of his strength and support. She looked up at her sister. "So you know how I figured out that Ruby Lee aka Lee Rugby was actually Ruthie Lee Rutherford, the temp working in the admin pool? Paul was able to fill in the rest of the story about her history. The history he thought he knew, anyway."

"What does that mean?" Meeks asked.

Farrah reached behind her back and retrieved several pieces of paper from her back pocket. "I ran a background check on Ms. Ruthie and the results were surprising. The background check revealed that Ruthie Lee Rutherford had, in fact, been married before…to a Walker Blackwell. They had one child together, a little girl. It seems Mr. Blackwell had trouble keeping a job, so Ms. Ruthie went to work for a temp agency that placed her here."

"Let me guess," Robert said. "That's when she met the love of her life—Ted Jefferson."

Farrah nodded. "Not long after she was hired full-time here, she was working as Ted's executive assistant. They had an affair and she left her family to be with him."

Francine gasped, her hands protectively covering her stomach. "She left her family…her *child*," she said, frowning.

"You sure about this?" Meeks asked.

Farrah handed him the report. "That's a summary of the background check. The full report is upstairs. As you can see, their marriage license and daughter's birth certificate are attached. I also have a copy of their divorce decree upstairs."

Meeks dropped the attachments on the table and scanned through the report. "Okay, I still don't see what any of this has to do with what's going on here," Francine said.

"Skip to the last paragraph on the last page," Farrah said to Meeks.

Meeks complied, flipped to the last page and began to read. "Ruthie Lee Rutherford has been residing at a senior rehabilitation facility for the past three years as the result of a massive stroke."

"My God…poor thing." Francine closed her eyes briefly. "Wait, so she couldn't have been behind any of this."

Farrah shook her head. "No, *she* couldn't, but someone has been using her name and information."

"You're thinking identity theft?" Robert asked Farrah.

"Maybe, but whoever's doing this had to know about Ruthie Lee Rutherford's history and her connection to our organization." Farrah's gaze moved between Meeks, Robert and Francine. "It has to be related somehow. This all can't be a coincidence."

"I agree, but why involve Ruthie Lee Rutherford in the first place? What could she possibly have to do with any of this?" Francine questioned.

"Let me see those," Robert said, reaching for the documents that lay before him. He first studied the marriage license and then the daughter's birth certificate. "Meeks, man, you need to take a look at this."

"What is it?" Farrah saw the color drain from Robert's face.

"What?" Meeks took the documents from Robert's hand. "What do you…?"

"Meeks…" Francine hedged.

"You see it, too, right?" Robert asked Meeks.

"Yes."

"What the hell's going on?" Farrah demanded.

"The child's name on the birth certificate is Jasmine Lee Blackwell," Robert said, squeezing Farrah's hand again.

Farrah took a couple of seconds before things fell into place for her. "As in Jasmine Black. Blackwell was her name before she changed it."

Chapter 27

Robert could feel the slight tremble that Farrah's body made at the sound of Jasmine's name. The sisters shared a look before reaching for each other's hands. Robert released Farrah's right hand and cupped her face. "Baby, no matter what Jasmine's involvement may be, she'll never hurt you," Robert reassured.

"I'm not the one she tried to kill." Farrah turned to find Meeks making a similar declaration.

"You're safe. You know that, right?" Meeks asked as he slowly ran the back of his hand down the side of Francine's face.

Francine covered his hand with hers. "Of course I am. Between you and all the security around me, not to mention that Jasmine was denied bail and is in jail—probably somewhere trading secrets with Alexia—I'm perfectly safe." Meeks gave Francine a quick kiss before turning his attention back to Robert and Farrah.

"So Jasmine Black is Ruthie Lee Rutherford's child. The child she abandoned for a man who never left his wife for her. Is that what we're saying?" Farrah asked.

"Yes," Robert said.

"Are we sure about this? I mean, I know we don't deal in coincidence, but…"

"Farrah's right. We have to be sure about all this," Francine said, looking at both Meeks and Robert.

A knowing glance passed between Robert and Meeks, which was followed by an accepting nod from Meeks. He sighed and kissed Francine on the cheek. "When I first met Jasmine, she was estranged from her father and she told me that her mother died when she was a child. After a year together she told me the truth about her parents, at least her *version* of the truth."

"Which was?" Farrah asked.

"Jasmine's father was a brilliant, unemployed artist. He worked odd jobs to make ends meet, and they did for a while…" Meeks scratched his chin with his thumb "…until they didn't. Her father got sick and her mother just left. Jasmine said she didn't know anything about her mother or where she was and she wasn't interested in finding out, either."

Robert nodded, adding, "Meeks told me what was going on and I offered to help find her mother, but she refused."

Farrah released Francine's hand, stood and started pacing the room. "So Jasmine's mother came to work for *our* company, where she met Ted Jefferson. They started having an affair and she left her family to become his—what? Full-time *mistress*?" Farrah said, tilting her head slightly.

"Sounds like it." Francine adjusted herself in her seat. "Ted Jefferson never married her. Even after his wife divorced him. She kept all his secrets and even defended him to anyone that spoke bad about him when Dad found out all the things he'd been up to. Hell, I'd be pissed, too."

"Me, too, but at him, not the company he worked for," Farrah said as she continued to pace the room.

Robert ran his hands through his hair. "Ted Jefferson would have a better motive but he's been dead for quite some time. Besides, whoever's impersonating Ruthie Lee Rutherford—"

Farrah stopped pacing. "That's it! She has the perfect motive," she said, staring down at her sister.

Francine raised her head slightly and crossed her arms. "She'd kill multiple birds with one stone—"

"And manage to keep her hands clean at the same time," Farrah added.

Meeks crossed his arms, mimicking his wife's move, and said to Robert, "They figured it out."

"They always do," Robert huffed. "Care to share with the rest of the class?"

Farrah turned to face Robert. "It's Jasmine. She's done it again. She set this whole thing up. Jasmine's been controlling things, even from behind bars. She's used other people to do her dirty work. Jasmine took her mother's name, so if anything went wrong, she'd take the fall. She hired Alexia for the hands-on sabotage work, while she supplied her with all the access codes and bogus documents that she needed."

"But how did she get the codes to your safe?" Meeks asked.

"I haven't figured that part out yet," Farrah admitted.

"I have," Robert said, getting up from his seat and going to stand next to Farrah. "Remember, this is Jasmine we're talking about. She may be crazy, but she's brilliant, too. If she was hell-bent on seeking revenge against all she believed wronged her, she would've found her mother, reconnected with her and somehow got her to share all the information, including intimate details that she needed to make her plan work, and get that back-door code."

"Backdoor code?" Francine asked, her brow knitting together.

"Most programmers leave a backdoor for themselves so they can get back into any system they've worked on. And remember, Ted Jefferson programmed all the safes in the early days. It's safe to assume that he kept a list somewhere that Ruthie would have access to."

"But how would Jasmine know that Ms. Ruthie would even know the code—or backdoor code—to the safe in Farrah's office?" Francine questioned with a doubtful look on her face.

"Because that wasn't always Farrah's office," Meeks reminded his wife.

"It was Richie's office first. When we upgraded the security systems, we changed out all the safes after you both joined the company," Robert explained, glancing between both women. "Your offices were the only two that *didn't* get replaced."

"Why?" Farrah asked.

"Your dad didn't want to replace those antique safes, so for additional security, we just added a ten-digit key pad to the safe. However, it could still be overwritten by a backdoor code," Robert said.

"Dad and his antiques," Francine said, shaking her head.

"All right, so let's say Jasmine was behind everything. What's her motive?" Francine looked up at Meeks. "I know she wanted me out of the picture so she could have you, but this goes way beyond that."

"I agree," Meeks said. "Jasmine may have hated her mother for leaving her, but she would have hated Ted Jefferson more if she thought he'd only been using her mother, especially after she'd given up everything for him. If she thought that his loyalty lay not with her mother, but with a company that she believed had done them both wrong—"

"Yet he continued to do business with us and remained a friend to the company until he died," Francine reminded them.

Farrah nodded. "If she had the opportunity to hurt the people she thought were to blame for her lot in life, including breaking up her family, she would—without hesitation."

"Add the benefit of destroying our company in the process, and that would be too good an opportunity to pass up," Robert added.

"So, how do we prove it?" Francine asked, scrutinizing the faces in the room.

"We show Alexia a picture of Jasmine and have her confirm and sign an affidavit stating that Jasmine Black aka Ruby Lee is the person who actually hired her to plant the false documents," Farrah explained.

Francine's forehead creased. "I wonder why she wouldn't just use her mother's real name if she was going to set her up to take the blame. Why use an alias…one so personal, at that?"

"She's twisted," Farrah said, with a smirk.

"No…well, yeah, but she's also a sociopath. Caught or not, she'd want *me* to know she was behind it all and why," Meeks said, shaking his head.

"Hell hath no fury…" Francine said, reaching for her husband's hand.

"Alexia's signed statement, along with the affidavit that Butch Johnson agreed to sign, should be good, right?" Robert asked Farrah.

"Yes but we'd really be in the clear if we had the forger," she said.

"Jasmine could've forged those documents herself. She has the experience," Francine said as she reached for Meeks's hand.

Meeks helped Francine to her feet. "No, she can handle basic documents, but nothing as intricate as Robert's designs. That would take an artist's touch."

A wide smile spread across Farrah's face and Robert could almost feel the pride that he knew she felt. Robert's right arm seemed to snake around her waist of its own accord. "All right, then who?"

All eyes turned to Meeks. "There's only one person that she'd trust to do it, too."

"Who?" Farrah and Francine chorused.

"Her father."

Chapter 28

"Her father is a forger?" Farrah asked, frowning at Meeks.

"Yeah, but he didn't start out like that. He was a really good artist—abstracts and stuff like that. He even had a little bit of a following. Then he became ill and had to take a break. Like any art form, you stay off the scene too long, people move on...they forget."

"So he took up forgery?" Farrah's head slanted slightly to the left. "What did he forge?"

"Government documents, passports, fake IDs..." Meeks said.

"Jasmine told you all this?" Francine asked Meeks.

"No, she didn't tell me any of it. At the time, she and her father were estranged," Meeks explained.

"I found out about it when her father got arrested. He called looking for help. So, I helped," Robert said. "I learned a lot more than I ever expected about the man."

"Do you really think we can get her father to turn on her? Do we even know where he is?" Farrah asked no one in particular.

"We know exactly where he is. He wouldn't turn on the woman who's been taking care of him for all these years. But we can count on him to protect himself," Meeks offered. "We need to make him think she turned on him...gave him up."

"You can't go anywhere near him," Farrah insisted. "None of us can. What we need is a very convincing attorney to approach him with an offer, and I think—"

"Hell no!" Robert barked, garnering both Meeks's and Francine's shocked attention.

Farrah offered Robert a sexy smile. It was ridiculous, but his obvious jealousy brought on a small sliver of pleasure. Farrah placed her right hand over Robert's heart where she could feel his racing heartbeat. She released a satisfied sigh and looked up into his eyes. "I'm talking about bringing Fletcher in on this," she said quietly.

Robert had either forgotten that they weren't alone or he simply didn't care. His eyes swept Farrah's face before he lowered his head and claimed her lips in a passionate kiss. Farrah returned his kiss with equal enthusiasm and was pushing him toward the corner wall when she heard...

"Farrah..."

They moved apart and Farrah stammered, "Oh...oh, I...sorry. I guess we should explain."

"Not now, we have a job to finish," Meeks insisted, obviously trying to contain his laughter. "You were saying that we should let Fletcher handle things with Jasmine's father."

"Fletcher can help broker a deal with the DA to offer him immunity on any forgery charges." Farrah pushed a few wayward hairs behind her ears. "Then he can approach her father with an offer he won't be able to refuse, especially if he thinks Jasmine is trying to sell him out, which is highly possible when she's facing all these additional charges. Once we have that affidavit along with the others, we'll be able to clear our names and get this bogus lawsuit thrown out."

"Do you want to call Fletcher and bring him up to speed?" Francine leveled her eyes on Farrah.

Before Farrah could answer, Robert spoke up. "Actually, there are a few things that I need to discuss with Farrah." His eyes cut to Meeks. "Do you think you can handle it?"

"Sure, we have it from here." Meeks took Francine's hand and led her out of the room, but looked over his shoulder, saying, "We'll let you know when it's done."

"What was that all about?" Farrah asked.

"Can we go up to your place? What I have to tell you can't wait another moment, and we need some privacy."

"It doesn't get any more private than this," Farrah said, her head glancing over both shoulders.

"I'd like something a little less sterile, if you don't mind."

"All right." Farrah raised her hands in surrender. They left the interrogation room, walked to the elevator and rode upstairs in silence. Farrah had a feeling that these next few moments would change things between her and Robert. Forever.

Robert's heart was pounding a mile a minute and he felt as though the length of the hall from the elevator to Farrah's door had tripled. After he confessed to Farrah the lengths he'd taken to have her, he knew he could very well lose her, and the idea scared him to death. Farrah opened her apartment door and crossed the threshold. She turned to see that Robert hadn't followed her in. Instead, he was standing with his hands in his pockets, staring at her.

She smirked. "Are you going to say whatever it is you have to say from the doorway?"

"You are so beautiful," he said, his face devoid of expression.

Farrah dropped her smile and held his gaze. "Why don't you come over here and say that again?"

Robert walked inside and closed the door, only he didn't move much farther. He just stood there as Farrah peeled off her shirt and while he knew he should stop her, the minute her breasts came into view, his brain shut down. His heart was racing and his manhood was hard as concrete. Without a word passing between them, Robert followed suit and within seconds, they stood before each other naked in her foyer. Robert reached out to her and Farrah rushed toward him, but before he could enclose her in his arms, she dropped to her knees.

"Oh, baby…" Robert's head leaned back against the door and his eyes slowly closed. "Farrah…wait… Fa…"

Robert's protest was falling on deaf ears and he knew that if he didn't want the moment to end too soon, he had to stop her. He pushed against Farrah's shoulders and extricated himself. He joined her on the floor and kissed every inch of her body before making love to her as if it was their last time.

"Wow…"

"Wow is right," Robert said.

"I think we should take this to the bedroom, but I don't think I can move." Farrah laughed.

Robert was up and had Farrah in his arms. "Your wish

is my command," he said, enjoying the feel of her naked body in his arms.

He gave her a quick kiss on her temple as he made his way to the bedroom. As he passed the end table, he noticed that the familiar manila envelope that had recently been there was now gone. Since Farrah hadn't killed him, Robert figured that she hadn't examined the documents yet or they were even better than Fletcher originally thought. Robert bypassed the bed and walked right into her massive shower where they made love again.

Bing... Bing... Bing.

"What's that?" Farrah asked, raising her head off Robert's chest. They'd only just made it back to the bed.

"It's a text." He reached for his phone. "Fletcher pulled in some favors and was able to get the DA to agree not to bring forgery charges against Jasmine's father. As long as he tells us everything, provides us with any and all supporting documents and testifies against Jasmine, he'll remain a free man. I have no doubt that Fletcher will be able to convince her father to accept the deal."

Farrah laid her head back against Robert's chest. "That's great. Looks like the authorities want Jasmine almost as bad as we do."

"I think you're right. Fletcher's flying out to South Carolina tomorrow morning to present the deal."

"You know, if you wanted to make love to me all afternoon, all you had to do was say so. You didn't have to make up an excuse. Anyway, I think everyone knows we're together by now. No more secrets. Thank goodness. We both know how much they can hurt a relationship."

Robert stiffened, feeling more as if he'd just been hit in the chest. He slid from under Farrah and got out of the bed. "Where are you going?" Farrah asked, reaching for the sheet to bring it to her breasts.

"I'm going to go get dressed. I didn't make up an excuse. There really is something important I need to discuss with you, but we got…distracted. Every time I try, we get distracted. Can you please get dressed and meet me in the living room? I'll pour us a drink."

"All right."

Robert selected two goblets and a bottle of Chardonnay that Farrah had in the fridge. He filled both glasses and brought them into the living room, where he placed them on a serving tray that rested on the ottoman doubling as a coffee table. Farrah walked into the room, wearing a pair of black leggings and a multi-colored V-neck T-shirt without a bra. Robert grew hard. *Down, boy.*

Robert handed Farrah a glass and she took a seat on her sofa, Indian-style. She raised her glass, smiled and said, "To us." She took a sip of her drink.

"To us," Robert said before downing his.

Farrah placed her goblet down. "Robert, what's going on? For a man that just got laid—a lot, I might add—you look like you just lost your best friend."

Robert felt as though every ounce of air had been sucked out of the room, and he was struggling just to keep his lungs working. He pushed out a quick breath and said, "I hope not. Before you came along, Meeks held that position, but now that role belongs only to you." Farrah gifted Robert with a big smile and he began to pace across the floor.

"What is it? What are you trying to tell me?" she asked in a whisper.

Robert came around to stand in front of Farrah. He knelt before her, took her hands in his and looked into her eyes. "I'm in love with you. I love you from the top of my heart to the bottom of my soul."

Farrah sat mute but held his gaze, and that's when

he saw it. A single tear fell, which was soon followed by several more. Robert released her hands and cupped Farrah's face, where he used the pads of his thumbs to wipe away her tears.

"Does that mean you love me, too?" he asked, his lips curved upward.

Farrah nodded.

"Can you speak?" he asked, grinning.

Farrah sucked in a quick breath, then whispered, "Yes… I love you, too."

Robert pulled her into his arms and kissed her. He released her and held her face in his hands again. "There's something else that I have to tell you and I'm begging you…begging you…please let me explain. Because if you forgive me, I'll spend the rest of my life making it up to you. I swear. Can you promise to hear me out before you respond?"

Her forehead creased. "That bad?"

"Please…"

"Okay, I promise," she said.

Robert took a deep breath and pushed it out slowly. "Farrah, I…we…" He reached for her glass and finished off her drink. "Baby, we're…"

Farrah pressed her forehead to his and gave him a toothy grin. "We're what? Still married?"

Chapter 29

"You actually thought you could pull a fake divorce over on me?" she asked, containing her laughter as best she could. "I'm an attorney, for goodness' sake. Not to mention you used Judge Cutter to supposedly help expedite the process. The man hits on me every time he sees me at the courthouse. Every…single…time. He most certainly would have had something to say if he had actually handled my divorce."

Robert released a weary sigh. "This was all on me, so don't blame Fletcher for any of this. In fact, he tried to talk me out of doing it, but I insisted."

"Why?"

"Because I'd fallen in love with you and I was too afraid to tell you." Robert's eyes roamed her face. "When you walked out on me…on us, I wasn't sure what to do. All I did know was that I couldn't let you go. Then Lawyer Guy showed up."

Farrah lowered her hands, laughing. "I told you there was nothing going on between us."

"I know you did," he said, leaning forward and planting a quick kiss on her lips. "But I felt like I had to do something. Not to mention the fact that you still thought I was a playboy."

"That I did," Farrah confirmed in a hushed tone.

"Are you angry?"

"I was at first, but when I thought about the reason you would have done it, even though I don't like being lied to," she said, eyes narrowed, a smirk on her face, "I wasn't mad anymore. I just wanted you to tell me. When you didn't, I decided to drop a big hint."

"Hint?" Robert questioned.

"I brought the bogus documents home and left them out in plain sight the last time you came over for dinner."

"I saw them. I was planning to say something sooner, but I…" Robert ran both hands through his hair. "I knew how wrong I was. Lying and holding you captive in a marriage you didn't want."

"A marriage I thought I didn't want." She reached for his hands and kissed his palm. "Being in love is very scary. Not knowing where you stand with someone can make you crazy. While I can't condone your methods, you made your position very clear." Farrah released his left hand and cupped his face. "You love and want me and you're willing to do anything to keep me."

"I absolutely do, baby, more than anything," Robert affirmed.

Farrah smiled as she fought to keep her emotions in check. "It was a crazy thing to do. It's right up there with the way Meeks loves and treats my sister and how Paul and John fought to marry. Baby, that's my kind of love," she whispered.

Robert grabbed Farrah and kissed away fresh tears that she didn't even know had started to fall. "So, Farrah Blake-hyphen-Gold?" Robert asked.

"Stay put." Farrah walked over to the side table in her foyer and opened a drawer. She removed a small box and returned to the sofa where Robert was sitting. Farrah handed him the box. "Here you go."

"What is it?"

"Open it."

Robert opened the box and his forehead creased. "A business card holder?"

Farrah chuckled. "Men. Look at the monogram."

"F.B.G. Farrah Blake Gold…"

"No hyphen, either," she pointed out.

Robert reached into his pants pocket. "I think this belongs to you." He took Farrah's hand and slipped a wedding band with a large, emerald-cut diamond onto her ring finger.

Farrah stared down and gasped. "It's magnificent, but this isn't my original ring," she said.

Robert slanted his head slightly and gifted her with a wide, sexy smile. "It is and it isn't. I took your original band and had it altered. I wanted to keep it as a reminder of the weekend that changed our lives forever, but I wanted you to have something more because *you're* so much more." Robert kissed her hand.

"I love you…*husband*." Farrah leaned in and kissed him.

* * * * *

A desire they never imagined…

Farrah Rochon

PASSION'S *Song*

KIMANI ROMANCE

PASSION'S *Song*

USA TODAY BESTSELLING AUTHOR
Farrah Rochon

April Knight has realized her dream of becoming a celebrated cellist. And she's returned to the Ninth Ward of New Orleans to encourage the youth there. Years ago, Damien Alexander urged April to follow her ambitions. Now he has the opportunity to revitalize his old neighborhood, and he needs April's grace and charm to woo investors. Will they be able to help their community and answer the sweet, sweet melody of love?

Available February 2016!

The one you can't resist...

Lindsay Evans

Untamed LOVE

A winning bid at an auction gets Mella Davis more than just complimentary services from landscape architect Victor Raphael. It sparks an instantaneous attraction to the brooding bachelor that takes her by surprise. Ever since love burned him in the past, nothing has cracked Victor's calm control. Opposites attract, but can they also overcome their differences...and sow the seeds of a thrilling and lasting love?

Available February 2016!

"Every page is dripping with emotion, making it all too easy for readers to lose themselves in the story and fall in love with the characters."
—*RT Book Reviews* on *SNOWY MOUNTAIN NIGHTS*

HARLEQUIN®
™ www.Harlequin.com

KPLE4390216

REQUEST YOUR FREE BOOKS!

2 FREE NOVELS
PLUS 2 FREE GIFTS!

KIMANI™
ROMANCE

Love's ultimate destination!

KROM15

THE WORLD IS BETTER WITH

Romance

Harlequin has everything from contemporary, passionate and heartwarming to suspenseful and inspirational stories.

Whatever your mood, we have a romance just for you!

Connect with us to find your next great read, special offers and more.

f /HarlequinBooks

🐦 @HarlequinBooks

www.HarlequinBlog.com

www.Harlequin.com/Newsletters

⧫ HARLEQUIN®

A *Romance* FOR EVERY MOOD™

www.Harlequin.com

SPECIAL EXCERPT FROM

Ⓗ HARLEQUIN®

Hunter McKay came home to Phoenix for business,
not to rekindle her romance with Tyson Steele.
Can he convince her that they deserve a second chance?

Read on for a sneak peek at
POSSESSED BY PASSION,
the next exciting installment in
New York Times *bestselling author*
Brenda Jackson*'s*
FORGED OF STEELE *series!*

"I understand whenever a Steele sees a woman he wants, he goes after her. It appears Tyson's targeted you, Hunter," Mo said as she leaned over. "Maybe he thinks there's unfinished business between the two of you."

It took less than a minute for Tyson to reach their table. He glanced around and smiled at everyone. "Evening, ladies." And then his gaze returned to hers and he said, "Hello, Hunter. It's been a while."

Hunter inhaled deeply, surprised that he had remembered her after all. But what really captured her attention were his features. He was still sinfully handsome, with skin the color of creamy chocolate and a mouth that was shaped too darn beautifully to belong to any man. And his voice was richer and a lot deeper than she'd remembered.

Before she could respond to what he'd said, Mo and Kat thanked him for the drinks as they stood. Hunter looked at them. "Where are you two going?" she asked.

"Kat and I thought we'd move closer to that big-screen television to catch the last part of the basketball game. I think my team is winning."

As soon as they grabbed their drinks off the table and walked away, Tyson didn't waste time claiming one of the vacated seats. Hunter glanced over and met his gaze while thinking that the only thing worse than being deserted was being deserted and left with a Steele.

She took a sip of her drink and then said, "I want to thank you for my drink, as well. That was nice of you."

"I'm a nice person."

The jury is still out on that, she thought. "I'm surprised you remember me, Tyson."

He chuckled, and the sound was so stimulating it seemed to graze her skin. "Trust me. I remember you. And do you know what I remember most of all?"

"No, what?"

He leaned over the table as if to make sure his next words were for her ears only. "The fact that we never slept together."

Don't miss
POSSESSED BY PASSION
by Brenda Jackson,
available March 2016 wherever
Harlequin® Kimani Romance™
books and ebooks are sold!